# The Kissing Law

## Dr. James Paulding

Published by
**Heritageheim Productions**
9744 Elizabeth Street
Parker, CO 80134
Email: hepaulding@hotmail.com


Cover Photo: Michael Sheppard at age 17


Cover and Interior Design:
**Concepts Unlimited**
ConceptsUnlimitedInc.com
303-449-2907


ISBN: 978-0-615-68933-3   (pbk)


12     13     14     15     16
0  9  8  7  6  5  4  3  2  1


Printed in the USA

*Dedicated to*
*Doris Wilson*

*T*he graduation ceremonies were finally over and it was a mad-house in the hallways there in downtown Denver, Colorado. Ten minutes ago I had completed my valedictorian address, which I guessed had been okay since several people had favorably commented on it. I was now trying to locate my parents in the crush of people, while still wearing my long gown.

My mother and father had planned a special luncheon for the three of us in an Italian restaurant in downtown Denver, celebrating my accomplishments during my four years in high school. My parents were attending a concert this afternoon following the luncheon, which was why I was eventually driving my own mid-sized Ford back home.

The stress of my final exams and my valedictorian address have worn me down a bit and so once I was back home in my own bedroom I promised myself that I was now going to relax psychologically, give up all things academic, and become a 'mall hound' for the rest of the evening. Now have I ever been a 'mall hound' in the past? No, surely I have not, but I felt this was the night for a little revelry. At the moment, however, I immediately fell asleep and didn't stir until sometime after 5:00.

It was now early evening and I have met a young girl in Cherry Creek Mall who would soon strip my life of any semblance of innocence I might once have had. We were sitting a few feet away from each other in one of those open places where they served cookies, as well as coffee, hot chocolate and other drinks. I noticed how pretty she was and how she had been glancing over at me once in a while. I took the last of my hot chocolate and moved to an empty chair next to her. "Might I buy you a cup?" I asked, pointing to my chocolate.

"No!" she said without smiling. "I want out of here. Do you have a car?"

"Sure, let's go." I was actually winging it then, something I seldom did. We walked together to the Ford, which I've had for more than a year since I was 16.

"Take me home," she told me even before I started the motor. "My parents are vacationing in eastern Canada. We can do something, maybe watch a little TV." She lived not far from Highway 470 in a good neighborhood in Douglas County. I had long since decided to let her run the show. God knows where I'll end up by midnight.

We parked my car in a circular lane in front of her large home and she led me into one of the living rooms and we sat together on the sofa there. I casually had my arm around her. She had not turned on the TV. Within seconds she pushed my arm away, opened her purse, which was sitting on her right, took out a rubber and shoved it into my left hand.

"Wouldn't you like a kiss first?" I asked, half smiling.

"Waste of time," she said. "Let's get the hell to bed."

Well, that didn't take us long. Lying there together I still hadn't seen her smile. I decided to take charge, even though I didn't have much of a battle plan. But I thought we should have some kind of kiss, whether she liked it or not. I kissed the middle finger of my right hand and touched it to the tip of her nose. "That's the last kiss I'm giving you. Next time you'll have to fight me for it."

After that for my new friend and me it soon became pretty much like it was for everyone in the world, except we somehow got excited and carried on a bit too long. It must have been several minutes later when she pleaded for a bathroom break. I thought she looked a little pale. Finally, when she tried to make it back to the bed, she staggered and fell to her knees.

"Good God!" she cried. "What's wrong?"

"I'm not sure. Listen, come back up here. We'll talk." I tried to give her my hand but she slapped it away. "Look, maybe it might be better if we knew each other's names."

"There could be something wrong with you," she said. She finally managed to stand up by holding onto the bed.

"Sorry, I didn't know you wanted me to stop. I thought you were—well, anyway. But please, let me stay for a while longer. Come back to bed. I promise I won't grab you." I moved farther over on my side.

She looked down at me, still shaking her head. I was smiling up at her. She finally lay down on her side of the bed. "Don't you ever come?"

"That wouldn't have been a problem. I just didn't know how much more love my wild girl was going to need, so I put it off." I reached for her hand and she allowed me to take it. "Know what I liked best?" I asked.

"Do I get three or four guesses?" I can imagine her rolling her eyes now.

"I liked the kisses best."

"Sure you did."

"You climaxed five times. Every time you did your hungry little mouth lurched up hard against mine. Like you thought those sweet desperate kisses would somehow ward off eventual death." I gently squeezed her hand and murmured, "I enjoyed you so much ...Friend. By the way, my name is Michael Sheppard." I waited for her to chime in.

"I'm a totally crummy sort of person," she said.

"No, you're not! I'm fascinated by you. You just need to work on your smile a little. Then everyone would like you."

"You're full of crap! I have a great face and body, but the most hideous personality known to man. I despise the whole world and wish I could blow it up, one continent after another."

I laughed and squeezed her hand again. "When I leave, I'm going to put my cell phone number on your dresser. You might decide to call me." I noticed a bit of moisture under her left eye. "Well, what's this?" I touched her cheek. "Typical me, spend an hour with a girl and end up driving her to tears." I hoped this would make her laugh, or at least smile. She did neither. I gave her a kiss on the fore-head again, whether she liked it or not.

The next morning was Saturday and she called me just before 9:30. She told me her name was Roberta Simms and said she had to see me. I suggested a late breakfast at a nearby spot that served breakfast 24 hours a day. Roberta had no car and so I picked her up at her home. We sat in a booth across from each other. I noticed again, as I had last evening, her dark hair, her brown eyes and her flawless, surprisingly fair complexion. Perhaps it's only my youth working here, but I thought once more how lucky I was to have such a striking young woman interested in me. I had not yet realized how dangerous her situation might become should she ever stray beyond wanting normal energetic sex to something else.

"I just had to see you again," she said softly. "I woke up in the night and actually cried for a while."

"Well, that's a hell of a note," I said, grinning at her. "And you're blaming this on me?" I reached over and took her hand. "Please don't start looking back, Roberta. We're going to go ahead, slow and steady. Looking back bores me. I just don't give a damn about it."

"And you're saying...what?"

"I'm saying that I really did enjoy you last night. And I'm say-ing that pretty soon we should consider going out on a real date. How about it?" She nodded and for the first time I saw her smile. But I had not yet learned how quickly Roberta could become bored with her life and offer up dangerous suggestions that might scare the hell out of many people, including myself.

"You knew I would call, didn't you?"

"Yes, Roberta, I did. I took you seriously and so I knew you would call." We took our time finishing our breakfast and then we drove into the mountains and took a long walk. We owed each other nothing and so the relationship would probably work for a while. But it would not work forever and eventually I would be faced with the realization that this girl meant danger, that she lusted for turmoil in her life, and that she might not care who harmed her later, or how.

I soon realized that, although Roberta was a couple of months older than me, she was in many ways more naive. She told me she had no plans to attend college, nor had she any prospects for a job. None of the courses she had been taking in high school were pre-college naturally, as she wasn't planning to go, but these courses appeared to me to be aiming her toward a future in the lower middle class. I wonder if she had considered this.

I like music a lot, all kinds of music, including classical. But I soon realized that we would not be attending the symphony together. Roberta liked country and western and that was that. She did like movies a lot, mostly comedies or love stories, and that's where people would be likely to find us on Saturday night. She had never read a serious book unless it had been assigned by one of her teachers, and she admitted that afterward she promptly forgot all the characters and even wondered why the book was supposed to be so great.

Of course, we continued to take long walks in the mountains, and we visited the malls once in a while for fun. Little by little, however, I noticed Roberta was not hounding me quite so much to jump into bed. Whether this meant she had met someone else I do not know. I never called Roberta because I was certain she would eventually call me. And I had never used my computer to get in touch because I had little faith she could keep a secret from anyone about anything. I had told Roberta I would soon be moving away from home and living by myself somewhere near the university. She seemed interested in this news because it meant a private bedroom. Still, I'm not certain how long Roberta will be with me. Maybe not long.

I could not say I was really acquainted with her family though I had met her mother early one afternoon soon after the parents returned from Canada. I remembered her being a rather pale thin woman, not at all like her vivacious daughter. I was certain the mother already suspected that Roberta and I were intimate. Perhaps she had been worried sick about Roberta's sex life for years. At least that's what I thought that afternoon before we drove away 'en route to a movie which was probably either a comedy or a sweet, harmless love story.

It was late July, when I turned 18, that my parents helped me purchased a small home near the university, presumably so I would walk to some of my classes without burning so much gasoline. It had taken my father and me several hours to move in, and the only thing left to do now was mow the medium-sized lawn. We had a 10-year-old push mower in our garage and my parents gave it to me. The little mower is what I was pushing right now on a hot sunny day in the late afternoon.

My house is at the bottom of a small hill. The next house up the hill is not much bigger than mine, the third house is larger, and the fourth house is huge. I think there might be some money there. There are no homes across the street from me, as this area is taken up by a large park featuring a lot of tall grass.

Each time I turned to take another strip of grass I glanced up the hill. I soon saw a kid coming down toward me, probably going on to meet other kids for something or other. Actually, I'd first thought she was a boy.

When I turned the corner again I saw the kid was a girl, maybe 12 or 13 years old. She was wearing a Rockies ball cap cock-eyed and had a little glove on her left hand. I gave her a small wave and turned back to my grass. Seconds later when I glanced back toward the hill again a baseball was coming at me full bore just above my head. I caught it by reaching up with my right hand. The brat threw hard and the ball stung my hand. I gave her a hard look.

"Don't you ever give warning?"

She stared at me and then walked up to retrieve her ball. "I'm Kim," she said without a hint of a smile. "That was a good catch. Of course, you're tall, with a good build and long arms." She stared at my push mower. "Why are you using such a stupid mower? That damned thing is almost worthless. Here, give it to me. I'll finish mowing your lawn. We need youth working here." She tried to grab it but I was stronger.

"The grass is pretty high," I told her. "You might cut off a toe."

"No, I won't!" She gave my mower another yank! I finally decided it was safer to let her have it. She handed me her ball and glove.

She soon realized she had to make rushes at the grass. She hit it from four feet away and then cut three feet of grass down. Then she pulled back and hit it again. No hesitation. I think she hates the grass!

"Hey, College Kid!" she yelled. "Don't you have any cold beer or pop in that house of yours? I'll be finished here in 10 minutes." She slammed into the grass again.

I watched her for three or four minutes to make sure she was okay and then went inside for the pop. I walked out with a couple of cans of Coke and sat on my front steps waiting until she was finished. She came up five minutes later, wringing wet. She grabbed a can of pop but didn't sit down. "Can't we go inside where it's cool?"

"No, sit down here. It'll be okay, Should I open your Coke for you?"

"How old do you think I am?" She yanked the can open in a flash.

"Where do you live, Kim?"

"In the big house up the hill on the left. My parents are sort of hippie types. They're either screwing all day long, or stoned out of their minds, lying on the floor, or elsewhere." She took a slug of pop. "Don't mind me. I'm acquainted with every cuss word known to man." Her head bounced around a little now as though agreeing with herself.

"The hippies give me complete freedom to roam the streets of Denver at will, mostly with my jeans stuffed with $50 bills."

"Aren't you ever scared?" I said smiling.

"Why? I'm the real killer on the scene. I carry a luger. Bought it from an old drunk near the mall. He was okay. Actually nice. But right after he warned me about the dangers of the night, he collapsed next to a big square garbage container. I think he croaked there." She glanced over. "Are we going to be friends?"

I can't help laughing. "Probably, if you'll start cleaning up your mouth."

She touched her flat chest. "You know, if I had tits I would already be out there conquering the world. I'm plenty smart enough."

I'm frowning, but I don't say a word, though I doubt that she's carrying a real Luger around. I took her empty Coke can from her and set it next to mine.

"Now be honest. Oh, I know I still look like a boy, but aren't you already sort of fascinated with me?" She grinned. "There's nothing like a blazing fast ball near the head to stimulate a man's concentration."

"Let's stroll up the hill, Kim. I want to meet your parents. I think you've been feeding me a line of bull!" I handed over her ball and glove.

"It's good we go up. You'll immediately see what I'm going to look like when I'm 17. My mother is a drop-dead, beautiful blonde. That's me in five or six years. My father is actually not so bad either, except for being stoned most of the time." She paused. "What's your name, College Boy?"

"Michael. Some people call me Mike, but I prefer Michael."

"Naturally. He's the Archangel. God, do I feel safe now." She grabbed for my hand, but I pulled it away.

"Don't press your luck, Kim." By now we were 30 yards from her house.

"What's your last name, Angel?"

"Sheppard."

She stopped and stared at me. "What? An Archangel and a Sheppard? Jesus, if we went to a court of law they might let you adopt me, considering my untenable situation at present here."

I smiled. "Remember, I'm just 18." I glanced over at her. "Where did you get all your brains?"

"I'm not sure, but I already know I'm smarter than you."

I laughed, maybe agreeing with her, though I've already been awarded a full scholarship at the university here. We've reached her front door by now.

"We'll just barge right in, but remember my warning. I'm talking about sex!" Inside the house there was not a sound. "The walls are thick," she put in. She led me to a large portrait of her mother.

I looked at it for several seconds. "So, just as you said, she's beautiful, and she looks really young." I glanced around the huge room. "Where's the Luger?" She walked to a desk, took out the gun and handed it to me. At first I believed all her stories, but then I held the small weapon up closer and I smiled at her. "This is a toy gun, probably made in Germany."

"Yeah, but it has little bullets and they really sting. Some people in the mall take them seriously." She paused. "Should we race through the house screaming our lungs out now, scaring everybody?"

"No. If your parents come down soon I'll be happy to meet them. But this doesn't have to be today. And please stop running your parents down, especially to strangers." I gave her the gun and sat down on a sofa nearby. She replaced the fake Luger and joined me. "Do you think you can talk for a few minutes without cursing?"

"Maybe." She smiled. "While I was finishing up your lawn I counted the years between us. I figured you for 18, just as you told me. That makes nearly six years; Do you know what will happen to those years?"

"Sure. Gone in a flash!" I grinned at her. "But you asked me if we were going to be friends and I said maybe. Actually, friends seem fine. But the ages in history seem to repeat themselves occasionally. Last year in high school I wrote a 10-page term paper on the Nazi era in Germany. You know, thousands of those Kinder soldiers fought really well in the last months of the war. But their principal task was something else. It was watching and listening, reporting on their own citizens. Sometimes I wonder if we're not approaching such an age again."

"What grade did you get on your paper?"

I shrugged. "Never got to turn it in. A girl stole it from me and she turned it in. But she told me later she did get an A." I glanced at my cell phone. "Who cooks the food around here?"

"Well, the peanut butter jar is never empty. Want some?"

I stared at her. "No wonder you're so skinny. Don't you ever order out?"

"Sure. Almost every night. Pizza, Chinese, ribs. Anything anybody wants. Would you like me to order something?"

"No, I should be going." I stood up. "One more question." I laughed. "You seem independent. You're not the jealous type are you?"

"You mean, if someone began encroaching on my territory?

Um. Um. Let me think. Oh yes, I know. Father bought me a large set of old 78 records from the middle of the last century. They were sort of scratchy sounding, but lots of fun. One of the songs was 'Frankie and Johnny'."

"What happened in the song?"

"Oh, Johnny was fooling around naturally, and so Frankie went down to the corner and blew him away." She smiled. "I FRANKIE, you JOHNNY." I gave her a small wave and walked hurriedly down the hill.

Good God I thought. I have a pint-sized Roberta living four houses up from me.

It was two days later that Roberta called, suggesting she would like to drop by and see my new house later in the week. I told her that I would pick her up at her home and that I would have some cold beer available. Meanwhile I have registered for my fall courses in the university and prepared to begin hitting the books in a few weeks.

I have not spoken with my young neighbor since visiting her home on that late afternoon, though I've seen her ride by on her scooter more than once. Although she often glanced toward my house she has not yet walked up to my door. I have decided that Kim would not be coming into my house.

On Thursday Roberta called again and cancelled our date for that afternoon. I did not ask why, nor did I argue about it. I have plenty to keep me busy right now with an afternoon week-long workshop dealing with 18th century American History I latched onto, which usually meant an automatic hour of A to begin my college career.

Friday morning I was tied up helping my parents get to Denver International to make their overseas flight to Hawaii. I parked my Ford at their home and we took one of their large SUVs to make room for the luggage. My parents will be gone at least six months, something I have been encouraging them to do for more than a year. My father had three other employees in his small real estate office and so he was able to turn things over to them for several months.

Ten days later Kim knocked at my door and stood there, her face bloody from the nose down to her chin. She mumbled she had wrecked her scooter on a rough patch of sidewalk, just down from my house. I quickly grabbed a couple of paper towels from my kitchen, handed them to her, and told her to go up and have her mother deal with this.

For two or three seconds, total silence. And then, in a strangely small voice: "Could you walk with me?" She had hold of my right hand before we reached the main sidewalk. I was carrying the scooter in my left. We climbed the hill to her large home and she began pounding on the door. She had not yet turned loose of my hand.

Suddenly I noticed she had pressed my paper towels tight against her right cheek, doing no good at all, allowing the blood to run freely down to her chin. When the mother opened the door Kim firmly spoke right up: "I hurt myself wrecking my scooter. Michael walked with me." I nodded to Mrs. Worthington while prying my hand away from Kim's.

I walked down the hill shaking my head in disbelief; I did not believe this scenario. It seemed a girl 'stunt man' playing a minor role in a movie. Her meek little voice at my door, the paper towels unused as we climbed her hill, the matter-of-fact announcement of the accident, and finally, proudly: "Michael walked with me." Sorry, Kim but I'm not sure I believe you. I just don't know.

Ten minutes later Kim was back in front of my house again. She had walked down alone this time. "I know you're busy," she said, "but I thought we might play catch for just a few minutes. To take my mind off the accident, I mean." I noticed she had her ball and glove with her.

"How's your nose?" I asked with a smile.

"Okay. It was mainly just a nosebleed. Can we play?"

"Sure, of course. To take your mind off the accident. But I don't have a glove so you can't burn them in too fast."

"I want you to throw hard. You can knock my glove right off if you want to!" She stuck out her chin a little.

I did my best for about 15 minutes, then I gave her a wave goodbye.

I had received my one-hour of A with my history workshop earlier and the fall semester was now solidly under way. Because one of my classes finished up around 11:30, I often grabbed something to eat somewhere in the university area. I was having a grilled cheese sandwich and a Coke in the university cafeteria when I was joined by another young man, asking for permission to take a chair across from me. I suddenly saw why. There was not another place available in the entire room. He was carrying a tray with a chef salad. I motioned for him to sit down.

I had recognized an accent. "Could you be from eastern Europe?" I asked him.

"Russia." He held out his hand. "Paul Stipanovitch."

"Michael Sheppard, history."

"I'm a Russian literature major. Right now we're working on Doestoevsky."

"Ah, the Karamazov brothers. I read the book last summer. Dmitri was a wild man, Ivan wrote the Inquisitor poem, and Alyosa was a priest."

"I'm not much interested in the religious business."

I laughed. "That's because you have been influenced by a bunch of old communists. What area are you from?"

"Well, you may not believe it, but my area is actually cut off from Russia now. Kaliningrad."

"That was German East Prussia."

"Yes, the Germans lost it at the end of the war." He glanced around the room, and then whispered to me. "God, I wish I could meet a girl. Know any?"

I threw up my hands. "They're running wild all over the place. Grab one." I watched as he worked on his salad. "So, you're all alone in Colorado?"

"Been here two weeks. Don't know a soul."

I stood up. "Listen, I have to go now, but if you see me here again feel free to join me. We'll discuss Russian literature."

Stipanovitch nodded without much enthusiasm. "Too bad you don't have a girlfriend who has a gorgeous sister," he said. I waved to him as I walked away.

Roberta called again on Thursday and asked if she could visit my new place. I told her sure, that I would pick her up at her home. Today would be the first time she had been in my small house. We had naturally needed a bed. When we finally drove up, there was Kim, standing there, her right foot resting on her scooter. She was looking Roberta up and down with disdain. I gave Kim a small nod and then took Roberta inside my house.

"Does that brat ever stare in your windows?"

"Not that I know of." We were both undressing.

"That kid's in love with you, Mike, and she already hates me. Better consider moving 20 or so miles away. Stay here and she'll nab you."

"Not at the age of 12 she won't. Come over here on my side, Roberta. God, I've missed you!"

When we left my house an hour later, Kim was still standing there. It appeared she had not moved an inch. I nodded to her again and walked Roberta to my car. I opened the door for her, but when I closed the door and turned to walk around to my side, a baseball slammed into the side of my head with full force! It almost knocked me out! I called back to Kim. "I guess you must enjoy hurting someone you love." I was hoping to shake her up a little.

"Shouldn't you be giving me a few swats? Sort of in revenge?"

"No, but I think you ought to be considering our entire relationship." I shook my head in disgust.

"Oh, and when might the two of you be leaving?" Kim asked deadpan. "My baseball is stuck under your car!"

"Soon, thank God!" Just as I was getting into my Ford a patrol car drifted by, coming from up the hill. The officer parked a hundred yards down from us. But when Roberta and I drove away, the officer pulled in behind us. He followed us all the way to Roberta's house south of highway 470. Because the cop was right on our bumper I didn't walk Roberta to her door; instead, as soon as she was out of the car, I continued on around her circular driveway and headed back north again. Immediately, the cop made a 360 with screaming brakes, nearly wrecking his cruiser, and was back on my bumper again. Within half a mile I gave up and pulled over on the side of the road, figuring I was about to be arrested. Strangely enough the cop didn't even glance over, but rather roared around me going north at a high rate of speed.

The next morning, when Kim was in school, I called her mother, telling her about the baseball attack. She made coffee for me. She was stoned and called me 'Dude.' She continued expressing herself slowly, with large dramatic hand gestures. She told me I was a trustworthy 'Dude,' that I was the best possible baby sitter for a woman such as herself, because she always knew where her daughter was, namely right outside my house. Then she stood up and headed over to get me a second cup of coffee, but gave it up when she staggered against the stove, almost falling to her knees.

"Kim needs more friends her own age," I told her.

"Oh, just forget it!" she cried, still leaning against the stove. "Why don't you stop complaining and just enjoy your little ward! God knows I can't control her!" I walked over and made sure she was all right, and then left the home without another word.

Well, I thought, Kim could be half right. She might be a hippie, but there was no way in hell this beautiful woman was more than 25 years old. This meant she could not be Kim's mother!

The next afternoon Kim visited me after school. I stood with her on my little porch. I had never allowed Kim inside my house. "It really wasn't my fault," she insisted. "The baseball just sprang from my fist without warning!" Then she stuck out her chin. "The whole thing was mental, anyway. We're supposed to be friends. Friends should get hugs sometimes. I never get any!"

"No, and you are not getting any today, either." I closed the door in her face.

The following week on Friday I met Paul Stipanovitch at lunch in the university and invited him to a small get together at my home that afternoon. I told him I would pick him up on the corner two blocks from here at 4:00. I told him I had plenty of beer and even a half bottle of Vodka. I also told him he could meet my girlfriend, Roberta then. Roberta had already told me she was coming to the party and that although she had a ride to my house, she would need help getting back home later.

Earlier I had set up a small table on the east side of my house with three chairs. I had placed the beer in an ice chest. I left the Vodka in my kitchen, to be mixed with 7-Up, or something else, should anyone wish such a thing. I also had two boxes of crackers and had made several sandwiches. While my two guests were not going to starve, they might get tipsy. It doesn't matter. I'm their designated driver and I don't intend to drink that much.

I picked up Paul Stipanovitch before Roberta arrived, and when she finally did come driving up, it was in a police car. Although I gave some thought to this, I didn't question her about it. I already knew that my relationship with Roberta was at best tenuous.

From the beginning moments of the party, I saw that Paul was an extrovert and that Roberta might turn out to be a bit sullen. One of the problems with our trio was that Paul and I occasionally chatted about history or literature, while Roberta knew little about either field. High school was over for us now, yet Roberta did not yet have a job, nor did she ever speak of any other plan she might have in reserve. I kept hoping she might change her mind about attending college, but I doubted this would happen.

It was then that Kim flew by, heading down the hill on her scooter. "Who's that?" Paul asked.

"The demon of the neighborhood," Roberta said over her shoulder as she went into the kitchen for more Vodka.

"Kim is a kid who lives in a big house up the hill on the left. We sometimes play catch together. She loves baseball."

"Well, be careful. You do know what happened to Eugene Onegin, don't you?"

"No, actually I don't. Who was he?"

"And you don't know about a girl named Tatianna?"

"Name sounds foreign," Roberta put in, coming back from the kitchen with more Vodka."

"Spin us the story," I told Paul. "Neither of us are up on it."

"Okay. Well, Eugene Onegin was acquainted with a young

girl named Tatianna. She was madly in love with him. But she was only 12 or 13, so Eugene didn't take her seriously. He eventually went away and traveled around various places until one day...can you guess what happened?"

"I think so," I told him.

"Oh, God, don't tell me he rushed back to the twerp," Roberta said. "I hate these kinds of stories. All those young brats horning in on the territory of grown women." She laughed.

"But that's exactly what happened. He does remember Tatianna, and realizes he's been in love with her from the beginning. There's only one problem."

"Tatianna was gone," I said. "He's lost her forever. Good Lord, somebody should have composed an opera from this story. It's a believable tragedy."

"Pushkin, Russia's greatest poet, wrote *Eugene Onegin*, a novel in verse. Tchaikovsky composed the opera."

"They're all dead!" Roberta said with finality.

"Well, maybe," I said. "Of course, with millions of Russian men giving thought to young Tatianna once in a while, it could be she's still with us, at least in spirit." I took another swig of beer.

Roberta waved my theory away. She had been drinking some kind of Vodka mix since we've been here and hasn't had much to eat. I'm going to remind my guests that there are more sandwiches in the kitchen.

"Hey, you two, how about another sandwich? I made plenty."

Paul stood and headed for the kitchen, saying he'll bring more out.

Roberta nudged my ankle with her shoe. "He's no freshman in college. He's older. I'm going to ask him about this."

I shrugged. "Okay, but he told me he had only been in Denver two weeks." I looked past Roberta to the street in front of my house. Kim was pushing her scooter back up the hill. I felt a strange sort of affinity with this young girl, even though she was often a pain in the butt.

Roberta noticed me looking at the street and glanced around herself. "There's your little Tat Yan, climbing up her hill. God, I'm glad she's heading in the other direction. She's violent!" Paul joined us with a plate of sandwiches and a half glass of Vodka.

"So, Paul, what are your plans?" Roberta asked. "Going to teach Russian literature in a college some day?"

He hesitated. "Unfortunately, that's not an easy road. College jobs are almost unattainable these days and, of course, most high schools wouldn't hire someone to teach courses in Russian literature. No, I'm studying my Russian simply because I love it. Actually, my final goal is to become a high school principal right here in Denver. I'm a junior now and plan to continue at the university nonstop until I earn a masters degree."

I nodded. "This means you had to have studied some place in Europe earlier."

"Correct. St. Petersburg."

"One of the most beautiful cities in the world. Why did you leave?"

Paul hesitated again. "Well, I might as well admit it. There was a bit of trouble with a girl. We couldn't agree on our future. No, I simply had to get out of that city." He looked at me now. "So, what exciting things have been taking place in your lives?"

I answered quickly to keep Roberta from blurting out secretive items I would rather not announce. "We graduated from high school last spring," I said, "And I recently moved into my little house here. That's about it, except for meeting Roberta, which was obviously a high point of the entire spring and summer."

"Obviously," Paul said, smiling. And then came a strange gap in the conversation. For a person who was stone-cold sober, and working on only his second beer, my small lawn party appeared to be grinding ever more slowly into oblivion. Paul and Roberta spoke less and less and their heads were nodding off more and more. By now they were both intoxicated and I should be thinking about getting them home. Suddenly Paul sat bolt upright! I thought at first he was ill.

"Good God, I still have a paper to write tonight," he said. "*Crime and Punishment*. Thank heavens I've already read the work." He glanced over at me. "Could you perhaps drop me off at my apartment?"

"Of course," I said. I looked at Roberta. "Want to ride along?"

"Sure," she said numbly.

"Sorry to leave so soon," Paul said as I assisted him to my car.

We dropped him off in less than 10 minutes and I wished him well with his paper. I'm not certain what I'm supposed to do with Roberta so I decided to talk to her about it as we drove.

"You're welcome to stay with me all night," I told her. "But what about your parents? Is that a problem?"

"Oh hell, probably. I just have to get my own place soon."

"Why don't you come back to my place? I can always run you on down to your house later. Of course, I doubt that you'll be interested in being bounced around much. You've had too much booze. And I really can't imagine making love tonight either. I wouldn't know whether I was with a mummy or a zombie." I grinned over at her.

"Go to hell!" she said.

I hesitated. "I'm sorry, Roberta. I shouldn't be teasing you. Why don't you just tell me what you want me to do?"

"Well, I'm half drunk. I'll admit it. I guess you should take me to my house."

This made it easy for me. Roberta was going home to her own bed and I would give her the usual gentle kiss on the forehead before leaving her at her front door.

It was November and the weather had changed here in Denver, Colorado. There was 10 inches of snow on the ground and Kim's scooter had been retired for the time being. She now glides by my home on small cross-country skis. Roberta and I still meet, though not nearly as often as before, and like old soldiers, it is possible one day we will simply fade away from each other.

It was a crisp sunshiny day when my postman came to me in his role of federal civil servant and who, within half an hour, would have turned me over to the local police. I saw him from a long distance, coming down the hill from Kim's house. I had three envelopes to be placed in my mailbox for pickup, so I stepped outside into the cold air and left them there. I returned to my living room to wait for the 'clinking' sound of the new envelopes arriving. I had not locked my door.

I glanced out my living room window and saw two small cross-country skis in the snow on my lawn, even as I heard footsteps coming nearer to where I was standing. It was Kim, in my house! She took off her ski cap, tossed it on the sofa and shook out her hair. We were now facing each other.

"Today is my birthday," she told me. "Today I am 13 years old."

It had been a few weeks since she hit me on the head with the baseball, and I had long since forgiven her. So, this probably meant a kiss. I walked up, gently took her by the shoulders, and kissed her on the forehead.

"Baby kiss," she told me sarcastically as I was backing away. I hesitated then, considering. She was looking at me, waiting for her life to change somehow. Well, I'm damned if I'm going to break her heart. I gave her a three second kiss on the mouth just as I heard the postman's 'clink.' He had seen the last of the kiss through my living room window and, my God, had he reached for his cell phone?

Kim already suspected they might be after us. "What's the plan?" she asked me. "How long do we have?"

"Oh, maybe five minutes. Just remain calm." I'm still thinking about the kiss. How could it have been so much sweeter than Roberta's kisses? Of course, Roberta never wanted to waste time with kisses.

"You know, Kim, in a way our present dilemma is understandable. This same postman has seen us sitting on my front steps talking at length, playing catch numerous times in my front yard, walking together up the hill to your house, riding in my car to grab milk shakes and so forth and so on. He knows I am unmarried and knows the two of us aren't related. The kiss inside the house was probably the final straw. Although he's a bit too chubby to have been a typical Kinder soldier in the big war, he did the same thing they did. He reported us to the police. History repeating itself."

"Like you wrote about in your paper that was stolen." She hesitated. "You know, our kiss made me dizzy."

"Maybe you're just worried about the cops coming."

"Or maybe the police won't come at all."

"Oh, they'll come. We just have to stay cool." I heard a cruiser approaching. "He must have been right in the neighborhood," I said. The car pulled up in front of my house.

Kim looked toward the door. "They must think we're violent people here."

"Well, they certainly might think that about you, but surely not about me. I've never been violent in my life." The officer was pounding on the door. "You're a tough cookie, Kimo. Go open the door."

She marched forward like a soldier, but when she opened the door I saw the officer had already removed his cap and seemed to want to talk. He introduced himself as Wilson Cramer and the three of us sat together in my small living room, with Kim and me on the sofa and the officer across the room in a large chair.

Cramer appeared to be in his early thirties. He's just over six feet tall, good looking, with a pleasant personality. His brown eyes seemed alert, especially when he glanced at Kim, who he may consider to be a 'live wire.'

"We have a complaint," he began, smiling a little.

"The postman?" I asked.

"Yes, he saw the two of you through that window there." Cramer was pointing.

"I've never been in Michael's home before this morning. I just noticed the door was left open and so I walked in."

"You're the girl who lives in the big house up the hill. I often see you on the road out there."

"Yes, I'm Kim. Today I was on cross-country skis."

"Because I will probably soon be moving to another department, which deals with murder, this could be the last opportunity I have to give you some advice. First of all, I would avoid meeting in this home for any reason. If you're studying together, do this either in a library, or in your home, Kim. I don't think it matters what you do outside, playing catch, sitting on the front steps talking, no problem. Also I doubt if anyone will even notice if you drive around together. If you go to a movie or a restaurant just don't drape yourselves all over each other." Cramer laughed.

"Why do a couple of friends need such rules?" Kim asked.

"The reasoning may seem unbelievable to you. There is a strange boundary for a young man at age 18. Many people view him at that moment as an adult, especially as regards his relationship with a young girl. And so, I was asked to come here and talk to you. I have done my duty. Now, Mr. Sheppard, get your car keys and you and Ms. Worthington drive around for a while. Kim and I nodded and the three of us left my home together.

In the car Kim told me, because of her birthday, there would be cake and ice cream at her home about 5:00. I told her it was perfect timing because, until then, I had work to do in the university library. I drove her up to the big home on the hill, gave her hand a squeeze and we said goodbye.

After spending several hours in the library and having a salad in the cafeteria, I headed back to my own neighborhood about 5:00. I had been working hard on two projects in the university, one of which I hoped to complete in a few weeks. This project dealt with General MacArthur and the battle of the Philippines in the Second World War. The much larger second project, which dealt with The *Scarlet Letter*, a novel by Nathanial Hawthorne, won't be finished until sometime in the second semester.

At Kim's home on the hill we had cake and ice cream and talked a lot about the sorry state of the U.S. economy. Stan and Lorna Worthington also asked me about my parents, who were still in Hawaii, and who probably won't return for at least several more months. I told them they're fine and that I've already received a couple of post cards.

Nearly an hour later I was surprised when Mr. Worthington motioned me into the library. He lifted a bottle of scotch and I quickly held the forefinger of my right hand close to my thumb, signaling I wished only the smallest shot. As soon as we had given each other a toast, he cut directly to the core of our problem.

"We are having a rather serious psychological situation with Kim. I'm certain you're already aware of this."

"I know she's a lively young girl. I also know she is smart. Meeting in my house earlier today was a mistake. Kim had never been in my home before. Of course, she told me it was her birthday. That's why I kissed her."

He took another sip of scotch. "Our country is going through a strange phase of political correctness at present. Frankly, I don't know how we arrived at this state." He hesitated. "How much leverage do you feel you have with my daughter?"

"Probably quite a lot. I'm certain she has a crush on me. What's the main problem? School?"

He shook his head. "She's a straight A student. The major problem is her risk taking. She runs out constantly at night, often carrying a little toy gun, which is useless. She also has access to money."

"What would you like me to do?"

"I'm not exactly sure. I myself don't believe in corporal punishment, and my wife has her own set of problems. I guess my choice would be for you to become an 'early night nanny.'" He looked me squarely in the eye.

I smiled at him. "An 'early night nanny'? What would that entail exactly?"

"Well, it couldn't have anything to do with your small house down the hill. If the police knew the two of you were together inside they would be hammering you constantly. No, I'm thinking of using this home as your base. Play board games, teach her history, improve her English, anything along those lines. The main objective would be to keep Kim off the streets at night. I would pay you $20 an hour for your service."

"Interesting," I said. But I'm thinking, young Kim must have been a holy terror to have driven this couple to this state. "I've already become fond of Kim," I continued, "and would be happy to help in keeping her safe. My main problem is my university course load. It's extremely heavy. Occasionally, I have to go into the university library in the evening. You can see how a conflict might develop."

He was shaking his head, dismissing this. "That's easily solved. Take Kim with you. Leave around 5:00, get something to eat over in the university cafeteria or some favorite restaurant of yours.

Kim would probably view it as a romantic excursion. I'll cover all expenses, of course. You could teach her the tricks of the trade in the library. Then she could later research her own term papers once in a while."

I noticed he had been watching me carefully. Surely he knows he has, for all practical purposes, placed his daughter under my complete supervision several evenings a week. This might become a little old, I thought. Kim's in love with me and we've already been warned about an excessive amount of intimacy on our part. God, I can imagine Kim wearing me out as I continued having to fight her off.

"Admit it," he said. "Your head must be spinning." He laughed and walked over to a shelf on a bookcase. He took out an article from one of the Denver papers. I already know what this is. It's an article about myself, announcing that I have received a full scholarship to the university here. There's a large accompanying photograph. "I saw you when you moved in," he said. "I saw Kim mowing your lawn. I watched the two of you drinking pop while talking on your front steps. I decided right then you might be a godsend for us here. By the way, I also know you were the Valedictorian of your class."

I nodded. "I'm actually interested in your plan," I told him, "I need the money and I would like to help out with Kim. But we might as well face the future here and now. At the age of 13 Kim will be no problem for me. I consider her a lively Tom boy." I smiled. "But this will change. She will become more and more attractive, more and more of a young lady. At that juncture, we might need to reconsider our arrangement."

"Agreed. We'll go forward day by day. Now let's have a brief meeting with Kim and my wife concerning our plans. By the way, I should like for you to begin your work late tomorrow afternoon. And Kim does not need to know you're being paid." I nodded as we left the library together.

My attitude toward Stan Worthington so far is that he's an aristocrat. Physically, he is tall and thin, with blue eyes and blond hair, perhaps in his mid-thirties. He's a friendly person, though one who appears willing to take chances. Actually, I like him and I imagine, largely because of his money, he may be helpful in regard to my own career. And, of course, Kim's previous negative remarks about her father will be ignored forever, and certain other of her remarks as well.

The problem remained the young 'spitfire.' If I'm able to settle her down some and keep her doing well in school, Stan Worthington might be satisfied and keep me on as Kim's teacher. If I failed, well, Kim might soon become bored with me; she might then load up her toy Luger with those fearsome little bullets, and drive me from the house. I guess we'll have to play it by ear.

The next day Kim and I visited the university library sometime in the evening. Once there I familiarized her with the computer system and turned her loose. I have gathered up several books in conjunction with a paper I'm writing about the Philippines. Tonight I'm concentrating on the Bataan Death March, a violent march where many American prisoners died, and there was much harassment on the part of the Japanese guards.

Kim had pulled out a few books relating to the Salem Witch Trials and said she planned to write a paper about it for her social studies class. I can't remember whether they hanged the supposed witches, burned them or perhaps drowned them. I've always suspected that these witches were probably damned good-looking girls, and older women hated them for this reason alone. Men probably hated them because they were being rejected by the girls. Perhaps someday Kim may tell me what actually happened back then.

From the corner of my right eye I saw Paul Stipanovitch entering the library. I waved to him, inviting him over. I whispered as I introduced Kim, reminding him he had already seen her racing down the hill on her scooter. They shook hands and Kim returned to her 'witch' books.

"Jesus, man, you haven't been here at night for quite a while." He whispered softly. "Is this your young Tatianna?"

Kim was immediately on this. "Who is Tatianna?"

"A beautiful young Russian girl who was madly in love with...who was he Paul? I've forgotten his name."

"Eugene Onegin. He made a drastic mistake about the girl. He didn't take her seriously at first and he finally lost her. Something written by Pushkin, our greatest poet."

"How old was the girl?" Kim asked.

"Oh, maybe 12 or 13. Onegin didn't see the light until it was way too late."

"What do you study here in the university?" Kim asked again.

"Russian literature. Actually, though I eventually plan to become a high school principal here in Denver." Kim nodded and returned to her books.

"How are you making it here, Paul. How are your classes going?"

"No problem. After all, I'm a Russian. How difficult can it be, studying my own language?"

"When do you plan to graduate? The spring? The end of the summer?"

"The spring, I'm hoping. But you do know I'm just plunging right on ahead, working on an M.A. degree. There will be no let up at all."

"Do you ever hear anything from that girl in St. Petersburg?"

Paul hesitated. "She doesn't know where I am. She can't know."

"Okay then, I'll just let it rest."

Kim has perked up. "So, there's another girl on the scene in Russia besides young Tatianna?"

I gave her a signal to cool it. "I believe that's over now, Kim.

Life is sometimes so complicated certain situations just can't be salvaged."

"You've stated it correctly," Paul said. "A situation that could not be salvaged. Well, must take off. Glad we got to say hello."

"Hey, Paul, check the cafeteria one of these days around noon. Maybe we can have lunch together."

"I'll do it for sure. You can teach me a little more history." He waved to us and walked briskly from the library.

Kim whispered to me as soon as he was gone. "One of the times when you were glancing over at me, Paul was looking by you, giving me a great big wink."

"Maybe he was just being friendly."

"Maybe. But it seemed strange. Also, there's something weird about that girl in Russia. It's almost like he might have done something to her."

"Oh, God, let's hope not. He has enough pressure on himself right now as it is."

Half an hour later when Kim and I left the university library heading toward my car, I asked her how she had enjoyed our first evening out.

"Not quite as interesting as roaming the streets of Denver on my own," she said.

"Come on, Kim. Level with me."

"Well, it's a question I ask myself. I'm not yet sure about it."

"You're lying through your teeth! You're also lying about Lorna, the lady you call 'play mother.' Hell, she's barely 25 years old."

"Twenty-three, actually. So what?"

"Well, you might just tell the truth for a change. What's the downside?"

Kim smiled. "Michael, the archangel, demands the truth, yet Kim the romantic knows that often the truth doesn't matter. Only our pretending is important, Michael. I've wanted a mother badly, so I have pretended."

I gazed at her seriously. "Where did you get that phrase, Kim? About 'pretending'?"

"Out of my head. But I also read lots of books. Otherwise, at my age I couldn't discuss 'romanticism.' I wouldn't have known what it was."

"Sometimes you scare me, Kim. Not because of your sharp little mind, but because of your emotional makeup. The character of the young girl, Tatianna, who you liked hearing about, was created by the Russian, Pushkin, who died in a duel."

"So? And this is supposed to scare me?"

"Perhaps. I'm not sure." We climbed into our Ford. "Sometimes I doubt that you need any teaching." I don't start the motor. "Sometimes I think my main job should be keeping you safe."

"Or us working together to keep both of us safe." She grinned. "What do you hear from Roberta?"

"Not much. I guess you scared her away."

"She wasn't the girl for you. Just my opinion, of course." She hesitated. "What do you really think of Lorna?"

"I scarcely know her. I'm wondering if she might not have a drug problem."

Kim laughed so hard she almost choked. "Drugs, huh? You think, maybe? What do you imagine she's on?"

"Have no idea. I doubt that it's booze, though."

"I'm actually quite worried about Lorna. I'm fond of her, too, though she may already be beyond redemption. Let me know if you have any ideas. We should try and help her."

"Do you feel she's good for your father?"

"She could be, if she'd stay off the damned drugs. She should

dry out, then she should grab my father, ease him into bed, and snug-
gle up."

I laughed and reached for the ignition. When we were moving
I suggested stopping for a malt.

"Hell yes!" Kim said. "We need something to bring our
senses to a new high! Giant malts! Even if we make ourselves sick
as dogs!"

I laughed again and took her hand. I left the car in second
gear, letting it bounce along as best it could.

Nearly a month had passed and during these weeks my sometime friend, Paul Stipanovitch turned up missing. We had spoken
about meeting for lunch occasionally, but Paul never showed. After
many days I spoke with students at his apartment complex but they
hadn't seen him either. I have trouble believing he would have left
our campus without talking with me, yet it seemed this is exactly
what happened.

It was now early December. As I was preparing to leave for
the university just after 10:00 one morning, my cell phone rang.
When I picked it up I was stunned to find a Detective Wonderlich
on the line.

"We understand you are acquainted with a young girl named
Roberta Simms," he told me. "You are mentioned in her diary."

"You must have bad news for me, Detective."

"I'm afraid so. Your friend, Roberta, has disappeared. She's
been gone for at least three days. Her parents alerted my department
after they failed to locate their daughter. We're attempting to find
everyone who knew her in the past." He hesitated for an instant.
"The situation doesn't look good. We don't need to go into that right

now, but I have a bad feeling about the case. Is it possible you could come down to the station and talk for a while?"

"Yes, considering this bit of bad news, I'll drive down right now."

When Detective Wonderlich joined me we shook hands immediately. He was perhaps in his mid-forties, slightly overweight, with thinning hair. "I knew about the diary," I said. "I knew I'd be in it, at least in the more recent pages."

"True enough. We found the diary in her new apartment."

"I didn't know about her apartment," I said. I took a deep breath. "I don't know what kind of information might help you, but if this statement could be somewhat off the record, I'll tell you now that, during the several weeks I knew Roberta, I was well aware she wasn't the brightest student in our high school. I didn't love Roberta, Detective, but I was fascinated by her. I suppose one could say she helped me grow up."

He nodded. "Give me a scenario. How do you think it all might have come down?"

I didn't hesitate. "This should be off the record as well, but I really believe this could have happened." I'm shaking my head now, somewhat disgusted because of what I'm about to say. "I think Roberta and some man could have been having violent, dangerous sex. Somehow he injured her badly. He dragged her to his car. By then she was terrified. To tell you the truth, I believe Roberta Simms might be dead. Frankly, Detective, I've been worried about her for a long time. I'm sorry."

"I understand. Anything else?"

"Also, recently I've been of the opinion that Roberta was drifting away from me. Once, a few weeks ago, she cancelled a date we had. I had a feeling she was ready to break it off. As I've told others, 17- and 18-year-old girls often prefer older men."

"Has Roberta ever been in your home?"

"Yes. Twice, actually. The second time she was there we had another guest, this one from Russia. He was a male student at the university. I had the feeling they had never met before. This was prior to the time we had our first snow. It was a warm day and the three of us were sitting together at a table in my yard. You should know that, like Roberta, he's also turned up missing. His name is Paul Stipanovitch."

"When was the last time you saw this Russian?"

"It's been a few weeks. The last time I saw him was in the university library one evening. I've tried my best to locate him but have had no luck. I've found the situation strange. Both Paul and Roberta knew me, and they knew each other. Of course, he's been missing much longer. I suppose there can be no connection." I smiled. "I imagine I must be your principal suspect."

"Better hold on here. We don't really know how long Roberta's been gone. We only know when her parents reported her missing. So, we presently have two people missing here. Any chance the two of them might have been better acquainted than you knew? Perhaps they fell in love on the sly, and simply ran away together."

I considered this. "Anything is possible, I suppose, though I have no knowledge the two ever met after that party on my lawn that day. Roberta was introduced as my girlfriend at the time. But honestly, I haven't seen Roberta for weeks."

"Are you acquainted with any other person who might have wished to harm Roberta?"

I hesitated. "Not really. But there is one additional set of circumstances you should know about. The first day Roberta was visiting my home a police cruiser drove by at an extremely slow rate of speed, heading up the hill on the road in front of my house. Although I couldn't identify the driver of that cruiser, you should also know that when Roberta and I came out of my house about an hour later, the cruiser drove by again slowly in the other direction. He parked about 100 yards farther down the road. But when I was taking Roberta home and we drove by his car, he followed us. He was behind us all the way to her home south of highway 470. I thought at the time the officer wanted to know where Roberta lived."

"But you have no other witnesses to this tale except Roberta."

"Actually, there is another person. A young girl named Kim. She was standing in my yard with her scooter when Roberta and I came to my house, and she was standing there when we left. Of course, Kim could have been riding up and down the street in the meantime. I wouldn't know."

"Has this Kim ever been in your home?"

"One time. I'd mistakenly left my front door open. Kim just wandered in. It was her birthday. She likes me and hinted she wanted a birthday kiss. Not wanting to break her heart, I kissed her. All of three seconds worth."

"Think carefully now. Is there anything else you feel you should tell me at this time?"

"Yes. Mr. Worthington, Kim's father, has hired me for what he terms as an 'early night nanny.' Should I need to visit the university library in the early evening I am to take Kim with me. In other words, the father has turned over control of Kim for at least a few evenings a week. For this chore he has agreed to pay me $20 an hour and is also covering all expenses. Kim was with me in the library that last evening when I saw Paul Stipanovitch."

"Why would this family hire a young college student to take care of their daughter? Was she out of control?"

"Definitely. She has admitted this herself. She was roaming the streets of Denver at night whenever she liked, usually carrying a Luger look alike, which I later discovered was a German toy. Kim's mother told me on one occasion that I should consider Kim my young ward. She admitted she had no hope of ever controlling her. Look, I needed the money and I'm fond of the kid. And I can control her.

There's no doubt about that."

"And there won't be any more kisses?"

"At least not until her next birthday, which is almost a year away."

Wonderlich nodded to me, letting me know our meeting was over. "Naturally, we'll talk again soon," he said. We shook hands and I left the station.

A few days after Wonderlich mentioned the possibility that Paul and Roberta might have secretly been in love and finally left town together, I went to the registrar's office at the university for additional information. After explaining that Paul Stipanovitch had been a friend of mine, I told the secretary that he seemed to have vanished. I mentioned he had been taking a full load and that he would soon be working on an MA degree in education.

The secretary told me she was not allowed to share information with another student, however, she did glance briefly at her computer screen.

"Did you at least find his name?" I asked.

She paused for a few seconds. "Are you concerned that something might have happened to Mr. Stipanovitch? Should that be the case I believe you should visit with Dr. Murdock, the gentleman you see behind that desk there to the left."

"Thank you." I crossed to the door and knocked softly.

The man waved me inside. "What's the problem?" he asked, giving me a smile.

"The gentleman is Paul Stipanovitch, a friend of mine. He seems to have disappeared. He was planning to work on an education degree here and later become a high school principal."

Murdock had the name within seconds. "Russian?"

"Yes. I've been looking for him for days."

"Perhaps he returned to Russia. You know, the only course he took with us was *Russian Literature in Translation*. It's a huge class." He glanced over at me. "Are you worried about him?"

"We were casual friends. Frankly, I found his disappearance strange. You say he was only taking one course?"

"Yes, as I said, Russian literature. Do you feel perhaps you should talk with the police?"

"I already have. So far they haven't located him either." I offered my hand. "Thank you, Dr. Murdock. There's not much else we can do here."

Only one course, I thought to myself while leaving the office. There is something strange going on. Obviously, Paul had been lying to me. I thought of Roberta again, and the young girl from St. Petersburg. Perhaps the Russian girl finally located him. But why wouldn't Paul have mentioned this? I thought I was about the only friend he had on campus. Well, enough. I'm heading home.

I never entered my little house without thinking of Roberta. Although there was still a small amount of snow on the ground now, I remembered the bright sunny evening the three of us were together, the same day Kim had raced down the hill on her scooter. I'm happy that things are progressing well with Kim. As far as I know she has not ventured out in the night alone, and her parents seem pleased about this. I have dinner occasionally in their home, and I worked about an hour each evening, usually with history, English or perhaps a class assignment from that day in school.

It would soon be Christmas. I bought Kim a box of candy and her parents a basket of fruit. The three of them gave me a pound of exotic coffee of some kind.

I did well this semester in the university and have already enrolled for the coming spring semester. This time I was taking an education class (actually the same one Paul might have been taking, but wasn't).

I have not heard from Detective Wonderlich again. Had he received additional word about Roberta, I'm certain he would have given me a call. I have also not heard anything from Paul Stipanovitch. Perhaps I was not as important to him as I'd thought. I guess with the pressure he had on him he finally just cracked.

Once, after returning from Kim's house about 8:30 at night, a patrol car drifted by me going down the hill. I often think of the officer who had waited down the street from my house and had then followed Roberta and me right up to her parents' home. While I'm aware that police officers often have opportunities to put pressure on beautiful young girls, I had no knowledge that this happened in this case, though the cop involved was certainly crazy!

And then there was Kim. Surely I had not yet seen her at her worst. But on the surface, as we approached the next semester, everything appeared to be somewhat better. Kim seemed calmer and even Lorna Worthington appeared more relaxed, though her hands still shook occasionally. Stan Worthington paid me every two weeks, which kept me in spending money.

Toward the middle of January I began attending Kim's middle school two afternoons a week in conjunction with the education course I was taking. I was accompanied on one particular day by Gene Henning, who was presenting the second part of his lecture dealing with the life and works of the great Bohemian composer, Anton Dvorak.

Yesterday Henning had focused on facts dealing with Dvorak's life. Today he was concentrating on some of the music, namely the first section of the New World Symphony. He had given a great lecture, walking the class through the music of the slow introduction, then the allegro, including the development section and coda. His explanation of the sonata form was especially interesting. The music was well received by the entire class.

At the end of the session he asked the students if anyone had a question about this greatest of all composers from Czechoslovakia. Kim's hand shot up immediately. "I don't know if you want this brought out, but yesterday Mr. Henning told us that Anton Dvorak died in 1904. There was no Czechoslovakia until later, toward the end of the First World War, so Dvorak could not have composed music in such a land."

I raised my hand. "It could have been at the time of the Austro-Hungarian Monarchy," I told the class.

But Kim's hand shot up again. She reminded the students, as well as Mr. Henning and myself, that tonight is the first dance of the semester and invited everyone to attend.

When the class had left the room I told Henning not to worry about the mistake because it was one anyone could have made.

"That Kim's a smart little brat," he said, "but I won't be attending her dance!"

Kim had invited me to the dance the day before. She wanted me to drop by for a few minutes so we could have one dance together. Everyone in this middle school already knew me, so this was no problem. Still, it turned out to be a mistake. It made me look foolish and presented Kim in a terrible light.

I knew the dance was up on the third floor and so, when I dropped by the school just after 7:00 p.m., I stepped into a large lift to avoid climbing all the stairs. I pushed the up button and the big doors began closing, but Kim had been standing with other kids nearby and she jumped into the lift at the last second. I stepped far to the back and let her run the controls.

The second that big lift started to rise, Kim came back to where I was standing and kissed me on the chin. But when she went on tip-toes, trying to reach my mouth, I gently pushed her away. "Easy, Kim," I said. "We'll go upstairs and dance a slow one together." But she became agitated then and turned and jammed a button, which stopped the big lift between floors. She quickly returned to me and, giving an airborne lunge, smashed her lower lip against my teeth! Now we were struggling. When it became obvious that I was much stronger, she grabbed my left wrist and bit it so hard it broke the skin. Now we were both bleeding!

She was just a kid, but I had to get her out of this elevator. I twisted her around so that her back was up against me, and then pinned her arms against her sides. In our struggle we lurched forward toward the door. She jammed her forehead against a knob on the control panel and the elevator lurched upward again. She had stopped struggling by now and was resting quietly back against me. The lift's big doors soon slid open and we were out in the hall. I stopped her in her tracks and was ready to tear into her, when suddenly something bothered me. The lights in the hallway were only half lit and the sound of the band seemed far away.

"We're on two," she told me. "I pressed two."

"What in hell were you trying to accomplish back there?" I asked.

"I just wanted us to share something."

"What? Violence?" I noticed her dabbing at her lower lip and saw it was bleeding. I took a handkerchief from my jacket pocket and handed it to her.

"I can't go to the dance yet," she said. "Let's wait in here for a while." She pointed toward a nearby empty classroom. We went to the back of the room and slouched down in a couple of desks. She tried to take my hand but I wouldn't allow it.

It was deathly quiet there on the second floor and where we were sitting it was almost dark. From a window on my right I saw some flashing lights, from an ambulance or maybe a patrol car. The silence in the classroom was beginning to unnerve me. I was afraid of what was going to happen. I heard her take a deep breath.

"It was a mistake," she admitted.

"I know."

"I have to start thinking first."

"Probably a good idea."

"I wish I had tits!" she cried out, astonishing me with her change of subject.

I glanced up toward the ceiling. "Well, have patience. They'll probably be coming along, right on schedule."

She was looking out into the partially lit hallway now. "I wish we were the only two people left in the world," she said, handing my handkerchief back to me.

"Wouldn't help our cause," I told her. "You'd soon lose control and start kissing me to death! Then, after a while, there would be no one left except yourself! See what violence leads to?" We climbed the stairs together to the third floor. I wouldn't think of getting on that lift again. I kept my handkerchief pressed against my bleeding wrist until we reached the dance floor.

The dance itself was interesting. Because of Kim's lack of skill, we held onto each other's hands, giving her plenty of room to watch my feet. I continued smiling until the music stopped. The same girl, who had attacked me in the elevator for kisses, was now hanging onto my hands like a six-year-old, trying desperately to make our dance as nice as possible. Grown men should never forget that they are basically children after all.

Driving her back home I scarcely spoke at all. I have already decided that I have made no progress with Kim as far as her personality was concerned, and will soon need to speak with her father again, perhaps as early as tomorrow evening. When we pulled up in front of her house she briefly took my hand, but I immediately pulled it away. If she's unhappy with my aloofness, then she needs to change her own attitude. I coolly wished her goodnight.

The next afternoon when I returned from the university I parked my car in front of my house as usual and happened to glance 200 yards across 'the fields,' where I saw Kim walking toward me. I was ready to turn my back on her and go into my house, but something held me back. She was coming at a moderate pace and so I had no reason to think anything was wrong.

Still, I waited for her there by my car. When she finally walked up to me I noticed she was deathly pale. Now I became concerned.

"There's a body over there," she said, pointing. It could be that girl you brought here that time. But I really don't know."

"Come on inside! We need the police. Fast! What were you doing over there?"

"I got off the bus with a girlfriend and stayed for half an hour. But after I saw the body, I got out of those fields as soon as possible!" The two of us walked into my house, although we really weren't supposed to be there.

I dialed 911. "How far away is it?" I asked Kim.

"At least 200 yards."

"I wish to report a body," I told the authorities. Of course, now the probing continued on and on and on...."

The police came relatively quickly, however. I stood with Kim while she answered their questions. I had told her earlier not to provide any personal information.

"There won't be any hurry," she told the officers. "This person's been dead for a while. Earlier the body had been covered with snow."

The three officers turned to me then. The sergeant in charge asked if I had also seen the body.

"No but I'd like to walk along with the girl. I'll stay well out of the way." As we walked along I turned to Kim, "It will be a bad scene," I told her softly.

"I know that. I've already been there."

It was highly unnerving to be walking across a field toward a deceased young woman, one with whom I might conceivably have been intimate. In spite of the shock of the situation, though, my mind was already churning wildly. I thought of the slow moving police vehicle going up the hill and then parking farther down from my house until Roberta and I drove by him. I even thought of Kim, who threw baseballs really hard. The only other person who came to mind was Paul Stipanovitch, who had disappeared at almost the same time as Roberta. At that moment Kim took my hand, whether to support me or herself, I did not know.

As we approached the site of the body I would freely admit this was the worst moment of my life. However, when I forced myself to look down, I must confess I was not really sure. Because the face that was left was totally disfigured, I would not be able to provide a name for the corpse. I didn't see how Kim could do this either.

Although initially I thought of offering my house for the police, I immediately discarded this idea. We needed to get Kim home. She could answer their questions in the big house on the hill. One officer remained with me. He was a Sergeant Williams.

"And so," he began, "there's no hope of you being able to identify the body?"

I shook my head. "The face is too disfigured. It looked to me as though this person had either been badly beaten, or an animal had gotten to the corpse."

"Do you know of any missing persons from this particular area?"

So, here it is, I thought. I could be indicted by sunset. "I know of a girl who I've discussed with Detective Wonderlich. Her name is Roberta Simms and she has turned up missing. At the time I knew her, she lived in the home of her parents, south of highway 470 in Douglas County. I understand since then she's purchased or rented a new apartment. But again, I couldn't identify that body I just viewed across the field. So we really don't know if there's any connection."

"Why did the young girl walk directly toward you instead of heading diagonally up the hill toward her own home?"

"As she was just starting across 'the fields' she saw me drive up in my car. I believe she was looking for help as soon as she could get it. I knew something was wrong the second I looked at her face. Finding that woman's body must have been a horrific experience for a young girl."

"Anything else?"

"Not until I know who that is over there. To tell you the truth, I imagine I'm still in a state of shock. Oh, one more thing. A male friend of mine from the university, from Russia originally, disappeared at about the same time as the girl I spoke of earlier. Frankly, this has always seemed strange to me. His name is Paul Stipanovitch."

"Have you spoken with people at the university about this man?"

"Yes, but they know nothing. Paul and I were just casual friends, though I still can't understand why he left without speaking to me. Paul and the missing girl were also acquainted. Before the snow, when it was still warm, the three of us had a small party out there on the east side of my lawn. It was one of the last times I saw Roberta, the now missing girl."

"Okay, thanks very much. As I'm sure you know, someone from the department will need to speak with you again." The officer closed his note pad and left my house.

Thinking back again to the horror of several minutes ago, I remained convinced that my statement to the officer was correct. I couldn't identify the body in the field. I found it somewhat strange that Kim had been more certain than myself. She said: "It could be that girl you brought here that time." Strange. There had not been much of a face left to identify. Of course, it's perhaps silly to keep thinking about Kim. She's a strong young girl, but not strong enough to have moved Roberta's body 200 yards into that field.

But suddenly I went into a kind of delayed shock. Kim hadn't needed to move a body. She just needed to trick Roberta into following her. And would Roberta have done this, knowing the propensity of Kim toward violence? Yes, she would have, especially had she been told that I was hurt over in 'the fields' and that Kim needed help with the rescue. All Kim needed to do then was pluck a hammer from a coat pocket, kill Roberta with a single blow and walk away. I'm scared to death. Good God, Kim is the most violent human being I've ever known. Of course, she could have killed Roberta!

The question is, did Kim hate Roberta enough to do it? At most she had seen Roberta twice in her life. But one of those times she was standing silently with her right foot on her scooter for an hour, knowing full well what was going on in my little house. No one was going to fake out a girl as intelligent as Kim and get her to believe Roberta and I were sitting around the kitchen table having cocoa. No, especially if Roberta had come back a third time, I'm convinced Kim could have dropped a hammer into her coat pocket and then, after walking Roberta into 'the fields,' killed her immediately. No doubt about it, I'm scared to death!

I had already mentioned Kim to Detective Wonderlich in connection with the police car following us the day I had driven Roberta home. Of course, the police may not even consider such a young girl for the crime of murder. I'm getting way ahead of myself. We don't yet know if the female body in 'the fields' is that of Roberta. I know one thing. I'm keeping my mouth shut!

I stepped outside to check if I could still see any police cruisers in front of Kim's house. Unless one or two were still parked around on the east side, it must mean the police are gone. I decided to walk up the hill and check things out. As I strolled along, I remembered full well the problems Kim and I had just experienced at her middle school dance, problems for which I hold her responsible. Obviously, because of the discovery of the body, though, I will need to postpone the meeting I had planned with Mr. Worthington. Standing in front of the main door, I remembered back to the day I had first met Kim and we had walked up this hill together. After knocking on the door, I was invited inside and soon we were all sitting together in the second living room. To suggest that the atmosphere in the home was back to normal, however, would be a gross exaggeration.

Kim's father began the conversation. "This is a terrible shock, of course. Kim told us the murdered woman might be your former girlfriend."

"I said maybe," Kim said. "I had only seen that woman twice! And the second time was from far away." She glanced at me now. "That was the day Paul and the girl were partying with you in your yard."

I nodded. "That was quite a while back." Kim's face appeared completely normal now. It would be difficult to believe she had murdered someone recently.

"We're hiring a lawyer for Kim tomorrow," Lorna Worthington told me.

I stared at her, realizing how nervous she appeared. "I can't imagine the police have much interest in Kim," I said, trying to be hopeful.

"We need to be certain," Stan Worthington said.

Kim was smiling at me now. "Except for you, I'm suspect number one. I admitted to the police that I didn't like your girlfriend coming around!"

"Why in hell did you do that?" I asked.

"It's the truth. I didn't think that girl was good for you. Did you know she was also dating a policeman? I'm aware of everything as I ride those streets out there."

"Kim told us she saw this girl in a police cruiser more than once in this neighborhood," Stan Worthington said.

I was rubbing my forehead in confusion. "I can't understand why they would have been cruising around here. Until recently Roberta was living with her parents south of highway 470. When I knew her she didn't even have a car."

"That girl is dumb as a post!" Kim broke in. "The only thing she had going for her were her looks."

But how could you know that, I thought immediately. As far as I knew you had never heard Roberta utter one word. "We don't yet know who the person is in the field." I told them. "If the body is that of Roberta, then I imagine all of the problems are going to come crashing down on my head."

"No one could ever believe you smashed that girl's face in over there," Kim said. "You could barely look down at her body. You're just not the killer type."

"Neither are you, Kim," I said.

"I wish to make an announcement," Kim said in a firm voice. "I demand that no lawyer be hired for me. No lawyer is needed. If the police can prove I dragged this Roberta 200 yards across those fields, let them have me. Let them examine my hands. Perhaps they believe I pounded that girl's face to a pulp with my 13-year-old fists! Frankly, I doubt they'll even come by to question me again."

Kim's father took a deep breath and counter attacked. "I wish you wouldn't have brought up your feelings about Michael's girl-friend to the police. They may believe you didn't need to drag the girl across the field. They may think you tricked her into walking there herself. No, I believe we are going to hire a lawyer tomorrow."

"If you want to waste your money, I guess it's okay." She turned to me. "Are you hiring a lawyer, Michael?"

"No, though I think you should have one."

"Why?"

"To keep you from talking so much about your feelings. Your feelings are not the business of the police. You know how fond I am of you, but you can bet your life I won't be discussing this with some detective. The police also know more than you might think. For example, a certain detective named Wonderlich knew immediately that I had been dating Roberta. I've already met with him in the police station. Of course, if the body in 'the fields' should turn out to be that of my ex-girlfriend, well, things will get more serious immediately. Within days the police will be all over my house looking for evidence."

"Are you certain about the lawyer, Michael?" Lorna Worthington asked.

"I think so. My folks are vacationing in Hawaii and won't be back in Denver for months."

"I think you should tell my parents about Paul Stipanovitch," Kim said, "and also the story of young Tatianna."

"Especially the information about Paul." I looked directly at the parents now. "Early last semester I met a student named Paul Stipanovitch. He had just arrived from St. Petersburg, Russia where he said he'd been studying for three years."

"He had gotten in trouble with a girl there," Kim inserted, "and he had to leave. He claimed he hadn't even told the girl where he was going."

"What bothered me, though," I told the parents, "is that it seems he has also disappeared. For several days I searched for him without success. Finally I went to the registrar's office in the university but they had no information for me either. Back in the days when

I was dating Roberta, Paul met her too."

"He met her one time at that party you had in your yard. It was a warm day and I rode by the three of you on my scooter."

"So for a while you had two of your friends missing," Stan Worthington said.

I nodded. "A detective I spoke with suggested, since they vanished at almost the same time, perhaps they fell in love on the sly and ran away together."

"Tell them about the young Russian girl," Kim said.

"You mean the girl Pushkin wrote about? I'm not certain I remember that exact story."

"I remember it. The young man was named Eugene Onegin. The young girl he loved was Tatianna. He made a mistake and left her for a time. Then, later he suddenly realized Tatianna was the girl he really loved. But when he went back to find her, it was too late. He had lost her forever."

"That's it, all right. I remembered the young girl's name, but not Onegin's."

"More important was what Paul said that one evening in the university library, the night he gave me that great big wink. It turned out there was another girl in Russia, Paul's own girlfriend in St. Petersburg."

Lorna Worthington glanced directly at me then. "And you say this Paul disappeared at almost the same time as your girlfriend, Roberta?"

"Yes, it has all seemed strange, especially when one considers that the two people who vanished knew each other, as well as myself."

"I think you need a lawyer," Stan said.

"Why don't you utilize the same lawyer Kim has?" Lorna Worthington said. "It couldn't hurt."

"Well, if you think so," I said. "But let's have an agreement.

If the police don't come back and question Kim again, then I won't avail myself of a lawyer either."

Stan Worthington took a deep breath. "And so, I believe we've covered everything we need to for this evening. But we must stay on top of this situation. We can't let it get away from us."

"I agree," I told him. I shook hands with both Stan and his wife and punched Kim lightly on the shoulder. As I walked away from the home and down the hill, I suddenly realized that I was totally exhausted, both from shock and from being worried about Kim, and what she might have done in weeks past.

Two days have passed since Kim found the body and, returning to my home from the university, I found two police vehicles parked out front. They are no doubt going over my house. Not surprising really. They have evidently just finished their work because two officers were getting ready to leave when I walked in. In the living room I found Wonderlich seated on my sofa, appearing concerned. The other men had already gone.

"You're bothered about something," I said.

"First of all, the body is that of Roberta Simms. I'm sorry. Your entire home was pristine except for something near your garbage pail under the kitchen sink. It's a rag containing a small amount of what we believe to be blood." He stared at me. "Do you have an explanation for this?"

"Yes. It is my blood. I had forgotten about a minor injury I'd received weeks ago. Good God!"

"Indeed. Well, let's have the facts. Describe the injury."

I paused, then. I met his eyes. "You remember I told you about a second witness on that first day Roberta visited me in my house."

"Yes, the child from up the hill. What does she have to do with your injury?"

I took a deep breath. "Kim hit me on the side of my head with a baseball. There was a small amount of blood afterward."

"An accident, I presume."

"I'm not certain, though usually Kim hits what she aims at."

"Stop protecting this girl! She's already told one of our men she threw the baseball on purpose. She didn't approve of you taking Roberta into your house. She hit you on the head when you were coming out to your car." Wonderlich laughed at me. "And you deemed this fact to be unimportant? What other examples of violence have you witnessed in relation to this girl?"

"There was an accident with her scooter sometime before we received that first snowstorm. She bloodied her face quite badly on that occasion. The accident happened somewhere down the street from me. Naturally, she knocked on my door looking for help here first."

"Again, your young Kim admitted to our officer that she actually punched herself in the nose that day in order to get the blood flowing, to make you feel sorry for her. We're dealing with a young girl who likes being kissed, and who may be drawn to blood. Now I want you to give me every negative fact you can think of regarding this child. And please, don't' hold anything back."

"Oh hell! Well, I've already told you she was roaming the streets at night before I was hired to look after her. I've also heard her curse on occasion. And when she heard my name was related to the archangel she tried to grab my hand because, as she said, it made her feel safe. I didn't give it to her. On the day we met she threw a baseball at me just above my head without notice, and then afterward we were sort of fighting over control of my lawn mower. It's a small push mower and I finally decided it was safer just to let her have it. She finished mowing my lawn. Afterward, we sat on my front steps and drank a couple of cans of pop."

"Well, some of this is troublesome."

I met his eyes. "I guess that's why the family finally turned their daughter over to me."

Wonderlich hesitated for a few seconds. "How much do you remember about your Russian friend?" He glanced at his note pad. "Stipanovitch? Could he be hitting people on their heads with a baseball, like your young friend does? Seriously, tell me what you know about this man."

"I'm beginning to feel like a squealer. I didn't like talking about Kim, either. God, I don't have the slightest fear of this girl."

"Why not? Maybe you should be scared to death!"

I threw up my hands in frustration. "Prior to enrolling in our university, Stipanovitch attended a college in St. Petersburg, Russia. When I asked him why he left such a beautiful city he said simply that there had been some sort of problem with a girl. That last evening in the library I asked him again if he had heard from the Russian girl. He answered that she didn't know where he was; that she couldn't know. That's about it. Oh, earlier in the station I told you he had met Roberta at a small party I had given in my yard, before the snow, while it was still warm. We were sitting over there on the east side. Roberta was introduced as my girlfriend at the time."

"And was young Kim, the baseball fiend, also in attendance at this get together?"

"No, although she did fly by on her scooter once. When Roberta saw her later, pushing her scooter back up the hill, she said she was glad Kim was heading in the opposite direction, because she was violent."

"Naturally. She saw her hit you on the head with a baseball."

Three days later Kim and I went out for a couple of cheese-burgers and chocolate malts, mostly just to get her out of the house. Stan and Lorna Worthington remained concerned about the 'Roberta' situation, and I hadn't been sleeping too well myself. Kim had a lawyer named Ben Zuckermann, who I understood was forbidding her to be questioned by the police unless he was present. The police, however, have not attempted to speak with Kim again, nor have they talked with me since going over my house for evidence three days ago. I had wanted to talk with Stan about the fiasco at Kim's dance, but we had other weightier problems at present. The dance episode would simply have to wait.

Kim and I were eating our sandwiches in our car in the parking lot so we could talk more freely. Since finding Roberta's body that afternoon, I had watched Kim's face at every chance to see if she was under some kind of stress due to the murder. I've seen no evidence of stress.

"Nobody destroyed Roberta's face," Kim said suddenly. "Some animal did it, maybe a coyote or a hungry dog."

"How do you know this?"

"My lawyer told me. He's been in touch with the police. I also know Roberta was killed by some kind of blunt instrument. Maybe by someone who hated or feared her."

I glanced over at her. "I keep asking myself again and again what Roberta was doing in our neighborhood when she was killed."

"Probably hot after you," Kim said, after taking a slurp of malt. "Maybe not, though. My lawyer is convinced someone brought her over there in a car, by way of another street. The police seem to agree. No one seems to think she walked in." She laughed. "You should be glad. I saw your face that first night. You thought I had killed her, didn't you?"

"I was praying not."

"But you were scared to death about it. My parents are still frightened, even though lawyer Zuckermann insists I couldn't have killed anyone. I'm not mature enough."

"Good." I relaxed then and sucked a little on my malt.

"Why do you like me so much? I look exactly like a tall young boy. And I'm the jealous type. Don't forget that."

I glanced out my closed window. "I'm not sure about us, Kim. I think there may be problems lurking."

She squeezed my right arm. "Day by day," she said. "Day by day." She took her arm away then and changed the subject. "I wonder if they've given Roberta a pregnancy test. Surely they have. My God, if she turns up positive it will be a horror story. It will make some young man appear guilty as hell! You have to know you're suspect number one right now."

"Probably, though I'm not certain the police are focusing on me yet."

"Even if Roberta had been pregnant you wouldn't have killed her. You're too moral. You would have taken charge and married her. That's your personality." She sucked on her straw again. "That's probably why I love you. But Roberta was not the girl for you. No way!"

"But how could you know this? You'd never spoken with her. You just saw she was beautiful. She was certain you hated her." I laughed. "She suggested I move away from here."

"I'll bet. But now I'm going to share something with you I haven't even told my lawyer, or my parents."

"Sure you want to?"

"Why not? You'd never tell. And you'd never guess what it is, either."

"I think I might already know. I think you met with Roberta a third time. I suspected that from day one. Who brought her to our neighborhood? When I knew her she didn't have a car."

"God, you're smart," She smiled at me. "The police brought

her. This was before the snow and Roberta and I sat together on your front steps. It was an interesting conversation. She had come over to talk with you that day. She was going to break up with you."

"I can believe this story. But that means she had met someone else. Who was it? One of the police officers?"

"I had always thought so. Now I'm not sure. You see, since then I've seen another car. New and quite large."

"Was Roberta in it?"

"Yes but I couldn't make out the driver's face. By the way, Roberta said you were something special, but that you were too young for her."

"I can believe that story too." I glanced over at her. "Now that meeting, when you talked with Roberta on my steps, did she leave with the same police officer?"

"Yes. The same policeman drifted back down the hill later and Roberta got into his car again. That's why I thought he was her boyfriend,"

"Keep concentrating on this meeting, Kim. I'm already convinced one of these men she took up with killed her."

"Oh yes, Roberta said another reason she had to break off your relationship was because you were so much smarter than her. You were already in college, and she never planned to go. She told me she hadn't liked high school, and never wanted to have anything to do with school again."

"Anything else?"

"Well, of course, I also thought of Paul. He seemed interested in girls, but he wouldn't have worked for her either. He was in college, just like you."

"As I'm certain you remember, he disappeared about the same time as Roberta. The detective I spoke with asked a lot of questions about my Russian friend."

"But where's Paul now? You looked all over for him."

"Did you know he lied to us that night we met in the university library?"

"In what way?"

"From the beginning he was only taking one class. It was *Russian Literature in Translation.* Don't you remember how he told us he would be graduating in the spring or early summer? And that then he would be working on an M.A. degree? That was a total fabrication."

"I remember he said he wanted to be a high school principal."

I laughed. "Fat chance! Paul dropped the one class he was taking and has since disappeared. But I can believe he latched onto Roberta. That would explain why he didn't want to see me again. He had stolen my girlfriend."

"Didn't he tell you once he had to find a girl someplace?"

"Yes, preferably a gorgeous one. Or maybe he said, a gorgeous girl with a cute sister. Something like that?"

"What happens now?"

"Let the police take care of it. Please, keep quiet about it. We don't need any more problems."

"Of course, if tests come back showing Roberta was pregnant, I believe Paul would have killed her in a flash. I think he hurt that girl in Russia, too. Hey? Shouldn't we be getting out of this parking lot? The police could spot us here immediately."

"You're right, of course. But I'm not certain there's any place for us, Kim." I gazed at her seriously. "Don't you imagine we'll have to keep looking over our shoulders, no matter what?"

"Why don't we just skip out for a week; enjoy ourselves, then come back and give the world the finger?"

"Oh sure. Then they'll throw me in jail and you in a home for love-starved girls. You know, it would be much easier if you dated a 16-year-old. Eighteen-year-olds are just one problem after another." I reached for the ignition.

"If you don't shut up about 16-year-olds pretty quick, you'll get another baseball coming toward your head! And when we get home you're going to kiss me once hard on the mouth, so I can sleep peacefully later."

"So, kisses for you serve as a sleeping aid," I laughed. "Detective Wonderlich said you were a girl who liked to be kissed, and was drawn to blood."

"Oh, that's true, that's true. Just call me the girl from Transylvania," she said as we drove away toward the big home on the hill.

At the time we hadn't realized anyone was following us. Of course, they were.

We eventually parked around on the east side of her house. But in less than two minutes, I heard someone knocking at my window. Good lord, it's the same officer who had talked to us after the birthday kiss that Saturday morning so many weeks ago. I remembered his name was Wilson Cramer.

"You're both lucky," he told us after I'd opened the window. "I deal with murder, not teenagers in parked cars. Now tell your girlfriend good night and then join me down at your house. We need to discuss Paul Stipanovitch for a while. Our department has developed an interest in this gentleman." Cramer walked away.

"Because of the interruption," Kim told me, "I now need two kisses!" She quickly flipped around in the seat again and pulled my head down close to her. "God, you're a great kisser!" she said finally.

The detective was waiting for me when I drove up. He asked me if I remembered him.

I nodded and told him I thought he had given us good advice that morning.

He looked at me carefully, perhaps wondering if I'm up to the shock that's coming at me. After a long hesitation, he met my eyes.

"Well, let's begin with the bad news. Roberta Simms was

pregnant. This changes everything, of course. We believe you'll need to give us a blood sample. You can come in tomorrow if you like. Right now, though, I want to discuss your friend, Stipanovitch. Let's first go over what you related to Officer Williams the afternoon the young girl found the body."

Although my mind was instantly on poor Roberta, I tried to deal with Cramer and the subject of Stipanovitch as best I could. I took another breath. "I discussed Mr. Stipanovitch with Officer Williams as well as with Detective Wonderlich. Paul had told me he was from Russia."

"You and Detective Wonderlich agreed, I believe, that he disappeared about the same time as Roberta Simms." He glanced at his note pad.

"Exactly. But let's remember, at that time I didn't know the body in 'the fields' was that of Roberta. I also remember telling both Williams and Wonderlich that I had gone to the university about Paul, but that the people in the Registrar's Office could not help me locate him. Of course, I also mentioned to others that Roberta was acquainted with Stipanovitch, and that the three of us had a party out in my lawn on the east side. That was one of the last times I saw Roberta."

"After these many weeks, what is your opinion of Paul Stipanovitch?"

"I have a more negative attitude now. There was something he told me about a girl in Russia. He said he had to leave St. Petersburg because of her. He also insisted she couldn't know where he was now."

"Do you think he might have harmed the Russian girl?"

"I don't know. The entire situation seems strange to me. I mean, where is he?"

"And you've never seen him again?"

"No, though I've looked."

"What's the deal with the girl I saw in your car up the hill?"

"That's Kim, the same girl you met previously right here in this house. She's smart as blazes and probably has a crush on me. Of course, it's a little embarrassing to get caught necking in the car."

"What about her parents?"

"Oh, there's no problem there. I'm five years older than Kim but, unless she gets tired of me somewhere down the line, we'll probably get married after a while."

"Not all police officers deal in murders. Some are busy chasing teenagers."

"I know. It seems kissing has become a dangerous sport these days."

Cramer smiled. "Well, watch yourself. We'll see you tomorrow morning for the blood."

Cramer hadn't been gone five minutes when my cell phone rang. The man who called was Ben Zuckermann, Kim's lawyer. Kim's father, Stan, had given him my phone number.

"I'm told you've been meeting with the police this evening," he began.

"Yes, they just left. One man actually. We discussed a Russian friend of mine, Paul Stipanovitch. Paul disappeared about the same time as Roberta Simms. By the way, the police are asking for a sample of my blood tomorrow."

"Go ahead and give it to them. If you refuse the police request, they'll just figure you're guilty. If it turns out you're not the father, well, we're no worse off than before. Back to square one." He paused. "Twenty minutes ago Mr. Worthington hired me to represent you. I think we should chat for a while. Right now. Frankly, tomorrow is too late."

"What can I do to help? Have you been told anything at all?"

"I know all there is to know about the Russian student, mainly that he's disappeared. But I need to know how Roberta Simms ended her life 200 yards across the street from your house, with no visible sign of any sort of transportation. Now young Kim insists she saw Roberta in a police cruiser at least twice, but who knows?"

"I'll bet Kim is right. She knows that street better than anyone."

"I've also learned Kim has a crush on you, and that she disliked Roberta. But I have additional information for you. The police are questioning Kim again tomorrow after school in my office. Stan Worthington wants you to be there, not for the meeting itself, of course, but more for moral support, hanging around in the waiting room. He insists you bill him for the time."

"Okay, if Stan insists. Actually, it makes perfect sense for me to be there."

"Also, there is another factor in play here."

"Another factor?"

"Yes. Let's move more slowly now. Mr. Worthington has granted me permission to bring something to light, something out of the past. And please understand, this is for your information only. It is never to be discussed, either with Kim or her mother." I heard labored breathing now.

"First of all, the day you met Stan Worthington, his family was already in deep trouble. At the age of 12, Kim was running out of control on the streets of Denver and, surely you know by now that Lorna Worthington is a somewhat disturbed human being. Also, surely you had wondered how it came about that you were drawn into the family circle so smoothly, you a young student in your first year of college. You must have marveled at the pay, the meals, and the power you were granted over their teenage child. Yes, you had to have wondered. And what about Kim herself? Had you not occasionally considered her mental health? What about Roberta's death? Were you not worried at first that Kim might have killed her?"

"Now wait a minute here!" I said interrupting. "Kim told me this evening that you told her she could not have killed anyone. She was not mature enough. And as I understand the situation, it is only now that the police are coming by to question her again. Of course, I hadn't known this until you mentioned it."

"I presented Kim with a positive outlook because I didn't want to agitate her. Actually, I have not the slightest idea who killed Roberta Simms. You, of course, could have done the deed yourself."

"Let's stop this right now! I want to hear about the business from the past. What happened and does it have anything to do with Kim?"

"Unfortunately, yes. In the past few years Kim has attacked both her parents for one reason or another." He laughed. "They don't seem at all able to fight back."

"I gathered that." I took a deep breath. "The first day, when I spoke with Stan Worthington in the library there in his home, I knew instinctively that something was drastically wrong, especially between Kim and her mother. And I couldn't believe the father was turning over so much control of Kim to me. But then I told myself: 'young Kim must have been a holy terror to have driven the couple to this state.' "

"Exactly. A holy terror!" Zuckermann paused. "But her father saw from the beginning you might be the key to keeping Kim in line. He saw there had been a bond between the two of you from the beginning and he wanted to exploit it. He had actually seen his daughter mowing your lawn that first day from his house. Hell, to keep you employed as his 'Early night Nanny,' he would have paid you $50 an hour, and given you a full expense account." He laughed again. "But let's return to your present predicament. Tomorrow the police are asking for a sample of your blood. As I said before, march down and give it to them."

"Of course, I can understand this request," I broke in. "I never denied I was intimate with Roberta. Kim could have told you that herself. She stood outside in my yard with one foot on her scooter for an entire hour one day while Roberta and I were together in my house. I doubt that Kim thought we were inside playing scrabble."

Zuckermann interrupted immediately. "Let me make certain I understand this. You and Kim were already acquainted and yet she was standing with her scooter in your yard while you were in the house with Roberta? God, how did Kim react?"

"She hit me in the head with a baseball while Roberta and I were walking outside to my car. I spoke with her mother about it the next morning when Kim was in school. Her mother told me she couldn't control Kim and that I should just enjoy my little ward. In effect, she turned Kim over to me. Stan Worthington echoed her sentiments."

"Has Kim caused any further trouble?"

"Not unless you count a kiss. The one time Kim was in my house (except the day we discovered Roberta's body, and we were calling the police), was her 13th birthday. I saw she wanted a birthday kiss so I kissed her briefly. We were seen through my picture window by the postman, and the police came in less than 10 minutes."

"I think you might agree that Kim had some reason to dislike Roberta. Only natural, of course."

"I suppose so, though I've never heard Kim say one word against Roberta."

"Repeating myself now, are you at all concerned about Kim as regards the murder?"

"Are you?"

He paused. "Well, I know so much about the family. Naturally

I'm hoping against hope she's innocent. But there remains the one thing that puzzles me, and you've surely considered this question more than once; what was Roberta Simms doing in a field covered with snow, 200 yards across from your own house? Please consider this question carefully and see me in a couple of days...." I heard a click.

Good God, man, I thought. "I've considered this question so damned many times it's almost driven me insane!"

The following morning I found Detective Cramer in the station. He introduced me to a young woman named Kathy. "Kathy is the needle girl," he said.

I offered up my arm. Except for one tiny prick I didn't feel a thing. Kathy soon withdrew the needle and handed me a wad of cotton to hold on the spot. After placing a band aid on the cotton, she gave me a smile and walked away with a vial of my blood. At times like this I always worry about a mix up of some kind.

I went back to Cramer and knocked softly on his door. Although he was on the phone, he waved me right in. No sooner had I sat down, than I thought I heard the name 'Kim.' I figured Cramer must be speaking with Zuckermann. So, I thought, it's true. They're going up against the 'spitfire.' God, I'd hoped it wouldn't happen. Maybe Zuckermann though, can keep Kim under control.

Cramer replaced the phone and starred at me for a couple of seconds. "A critical juncture, right? The blood will not lie."

"I'm not too worried. I think I was careful with Roberta. Hey, I thought I heard Kim's name earlier. I gather this means she's being questioned again. Zuckermann's office, right after school. Correct?"

"That's privileged information, of course. But, oh hell, she'll just tell you later this afternoon anyway. Yes, the meeting is right after school."

"I'm with Kim an hour each evening. She doesn't seem the least bit worried about anything pertaining to the murder."

"Could be. Let's hope for the best."

"Who is doing the questioning?"

"Wonderlich. I believe you know him."

"Yes. He's very fair."

I paused for a few seconds. "Do you have any information about Roberta catching rides in police cruisers, especially to the area of the murder, namely near my home?"

Cramer was shaking his head. "Why would she need the police? Didn't she have a car?"

"Actually, she didn't, at least not when we were dating. Kim claimed she saw Roberta twice, riding in police vehicles. Many weeks ago Roberta and I had a strange experience. A police cruiser slowly ascended the hill by Kim's house, then, slowly returned, parking about 100 yards down from my home. The surprising fact was, when Roberta and I left in order to take her home south of 470, the police cruiser followed us right on our tail the entire way. I was convinced he wanted to know where she lived."

"This is news to me. Although I'd never seen Roberta when she was alive, I understood she was a beautiful woman. Perhaps the officer was just hoping to get acquainted somehow."

"Perhaps. Say, when do you think my blood work might be finished?"

"Three days, tops. And when do I get some help from you? When are you going to deliver Mr. Paul Stipanovitch to me?" We both laughed, because we have both pretty much given up on this endeavor, at least for the time being.

When I left the police station I went directly to my English class, which ran about 50 minutes. While driving back to campus I gave one last thought to my Russian friend. When my class was finished I decided to try and find a certain Vaslov Lermantov, Professor of *Russian Literature in Translation.* The professor had just returned to his office after teaching his own class. He also seemed to have a bit of time. I introduced myself and mentioned the name, Stipanovitch.

Lermantov nodded. "I know the name, but I doubt I'm going to be able to help you much. Paul Stipanovitch dropped my course weeks ago."

"Do you know anything about him?"

"I take it he's a friend of yours. Well, I know he came from a college in St. Petersburg at the beginning of the fall semester. He was broke and therefore eventually dropped out of the university here. I believe I heard he started working in a machine shop somewhere over on Santa Fe."

"When did you hear this?"

"Oh, about a month ago. I know he needed money. He was desperate."

"Did you ever hear about a girl he had known in St. Petersburg?"

"Never heard that story. You do know that my Russian literature course has an enrollment of more than 140. I've never had the good fortune of becoming close to many of my students. I doubt I would have remembered Stipanovitch had he not been from Russia."

"Kalininburg. He told me that's where he was from. Even mentioned his area. Said it was cut off from the rest of Russia."

"Paul Stipanovitch wasn't from old Prussia. You're mistaken here, Sir. Paul Stipanovitch was from Minsk! I should know, and remember. I just saw the man as recently as five weeks ago. Definitely Minsk!"

I was in total shock. "Five weeks ago?" I took a deep breath. "Thank you very much, Professor Lermantov. I deeply appreciate your help."

So, now what do I do? Santa Fe is a long street filled with some small factories and stores of every kind. Unless I can find someone else who knows where Paul is living, I'll have to go back to Wilson Cramer. Only the police would be able to mount this kind of massive search in locating a murder suspect.

At the moment I'm suspect number one, and Kim is probably suspect number two. Of course, had Roberta's body been discovered elsewhere, only my blood would have connected me and only then if it could be proven I was the father. The large field across from my house remained the critical factor in everything, for Kim, as well as myself. Had Roberta's body been discovered five miles away, people would have laughed at the thought of Kim as a suspect!"

I had already memorized the address of Ben Zuckermann's law office and I planned to arrive there even before Kim and her parents came in after school. I was actually following Ben's advice, namely the message he had given me from Stan Worthington. While I was certain I wouldn't be allowed into the room where Wonderlich was questioning Kim, at least I could give the family moral support when they walked through the door.

I glanced at my cell phone and saw that I had just enough time to visit Paul's old apartment on the chance he had moved back there without my knowing it. A young man my age named Hector Garcia, who I had questioned weeks before, only shook his head this time as well, suggesting Russia as Paul's possible destination. I nodded, thanked him, and walked away.

I found Zuckermann's office within five minutes, but was immediately made aware that the beautiful secretary behind the desk was not in a welcoming mood, at least not for 18-year-olds who were not a member of the immediate family. I came close to announcing that the young girl arriving after school today had been declared my own ward, but of course I didn't. Instead, I took a chair directly across from the gorgeous one and dared her to throw me out of the office.

Wonderlich was the next person to arrive and I stood at once and offered my hand. He thanked me for giving the blood sample earlier that morning and wished me well in the long run.

He was immediately invited into Zuckermann's office, no doubt to work out certain procedures. The 'spitfire' would soon be here. I was having some trouble keeping my eyes off the secretary and I was hoping my gaze was unnerving her just a little as well. I can't imagine how Zuckermann could concentrate in this office with such a woman around. Perhaps she was his wife, though I doubted it.

Ah, other people were about to arrive. Kim and her parents came in and walked up to the front desk. Kim didn't bother listening to the conversation, but rather stepped back to me. We gave each other a hug and then sat down together. Her parents joined us almost at once.

"Did you get to the station this morning?" Stan asked me.

"No problem."

"Did they poke you?" Kim asked, laughing.

"They took a couple of quarts," I told her.

"You're lying. How much did they really take?"

"One vial. It took about 10 seconds." I grinned at her.

I noticed the gorgeous one behind the desk was perturbed with our conversation, but we were interrupted anyway because Zuckermann exited his office and walked over to us. I figured him for 45, with blue eyes, white hair and yes, good muscle tone. He shook hands with Kim and her parents, but only nodded at me, like perhaps he might deal with me another day. He invited Kim toward him, but I still had hold of her hand and I kept her by me until I'd given her a good big wink.

"She seemed in good spirits," I told her parents later. "The detective inside that office is a soft spoken straight shooter. I don't believe there will be any problem." Lorna Worthington nodded in agreement.

"Is there anything new?" Stan asked.

"Actually, yes. This morning another detective named Wilson Cramer reminded me in a kind of joking way that it was time for me to deliver Mr. Stipanovitch to the station. We both laughed because no one believes this is going to happen, at least not right away. But while driving back to the university I considered my quest for Paul one last time so, after my English class, I decided to try and locate a certain Vaslov Lermantov, Professor of *Russian Literature in Translation*."

"Luckily Lermantov had just returned to his office when I arrived at his door. He was friendly and said he had time for me." I looked seriously at both Mr. and Mrs. Worthington. "Now I'm going to make this short. This professor had seen Paul Stipanovitch within the past five weeks. He reported that Paul was totally broke, and working in some machine shop on Santa Fe. But when I checked back later to see if the Russian had ever returned to his old apartment, I was told that people there hadn't seen him for weeks. Where, I'm wondering does this man live? Under a bridge?"

"Of course, he could be here in Colorado and still have nothing to do with Roberta's murder," Stan said.

"Naturally." I laughed a little. "But when a person is suspect number one and they're drawing his blood early in the morning, one looks to other people to share some of the burden of suspicion."

I glanced at Lorna Worthington then, trying to keep her attention. "Another interesting tidbit has to do with Paul's home in Russia. He had told me from the beginning his home was old German Prussia and even emphasized that the territory was presently cut off from the rest of Russia. Professor Lermantov told me that he was certain Paul was not from Kalininburg, but rather from the city of Minsk!" I laughed again. "One immediately recognized the lies. I'm also beginning to think Kim is right. Paul Stiipanovitch really could have harmed someone, probably a girl, and for months has been covering his tracks by playing one Russian city against another."

"Is it possible he's now been hired under an assumed name?" Lorna asked.

"Yes, and this is why tomorrow I'm turning all of this information over to the police." At that moment Zuckermann opened his office door, allowing Wonderlich to escape. The detective glanced at us, looking noncommittal and left the office without another word.

Zuckermann invited Lorna and Stan Worthington to join him in his office, but Kim rushed out past the lawyer inviting me to the meeting as well. I told her this was not possible and said we could talk later. "I hope everything is okay," I said quickly. She nodded in a positive way.

Later, in the Worthington home we met in the second living room and discussed the happenings of the late afternoon. Kim appeared to have a positive attitude, however the two grownups seemed less optimistic. We had ordered two large pizzas and were taking our time eating them.

Kim's father asked if there were any questions that bothered her.

"The detective asked why I hadn't walked to the right in a diagonal up the hill toward our house, instead of heading straight across the fields toward Michael."

"And what did you tell him?" I asked.

"That I had seen you drive up in your car and that I was shaken up from finding the body and needed help as soon as I could get it."

"Is there anything else you'd like to share with us?" Lorna asked.

"I had the feeling this Wonderlich person didn't have much faith in me as a murderer. He doubted I was up to the task." She gave us all a smile.

"Did the detective ask how you came to be on the opposite side of the park when, getting off the school bus?" her father asked.

Kim shook her head. "No one expressed any interest in that, and I didn't volunteer anything."

"Did the detective ask you about your feelings regarding Roberta?" I asked softly.

"Yes, he did, but my lawyer wouldn't let me answer. If you want my opinion, I doubt the police are going to bother me again."

The two adults seemed to relax a little more after that statement and I for one was ready for more pizza.

In the morning I called Detective Cramer again and gave him the information about Stipanovitch. I told him that Santa Fe was too large a territory for me to canvas and that it was also possible the Russian might have hired on at the machine shop under an assumed name. I added that I don't have the slightest idea where he could be living, but I know it wasn't where it used to be.

Cramer told me another person wanted to speak with me. I was surprised when I heard Wonderlich on the line. "Good news," he said simply. "You are not the father of the fetus. You should consider it a major breakthrough. But as for Kim, she's not leveling with us. I can't imagine what reason she might have for this, but she's holding back."

"But surely, you don't think she could have had anything to do with the murder?"

"No, not really, and I don't plan to question her again. Zuckermann won't allow her to answer the important questions, so it's really a waste of time. Do you have any new information dealing with this cockeyed case?"

"Yes. Just yesterday. I've already told Detective Cramer about this. Paul Stipanovitch is still in Colorado, as least he was five weeks ago. I obtained this information from a certain Professor Vaslav Lermantov, who teaches *Russian Literature in Translation*. Paul had been in his class but had dropped out even before the fall semester ended. The Russian was broke. According to what I was told, he is now working in a machine shop over on Santa Fe. I have no idea where he lives, nor do I know if he signed on for the job under his own name, or an alias. Perhaps he's living under a bridge. So, now you know what I know, Detective. I wish you luck."

"Do you still think he might have harmed someone back in Russia?"

"It's possible, though I have no proof. He mentioned a girl in St. Petersburg more than once. He was also running three different Russian cities as his home base. I believe he doesn't want to be found."

"Anything else?"

"Well since you gave me the news about the blood work, I'm more relaxed about Roberta's murder. Without a breakthrough, though, I doubt this crime will ever be solved. Of course, I knew I was innocent. After all, why would I have wanted to kill that beautiful girl?"

"Yes, I see your point."

"So long Detective."

"Good luck with the kid," he told me.

I called Zuckermann's office and set up an appointment for 2:30 that afternoon. He said he had half an hour or so. I'm betting he's already heard the report on my blood work and is probably losing interest in me.

Arriving at the office I found the waiting room empty. My favorite secretary was still on duty, however she's more friendly today, probably because I'm an actual client. Within five minutes she knocked on Zuckermann's office door and then ushered me inside. I still have mixed feelings about this lawyer, mostly because of his negative attitude about Kim and her mother, but I've promised myself to keep an open mind. After all, I won't be the one paying his bills. As we shook hands he was already talking.

"A good deal with the blood work. I've already heard about it."

"Yes, good, but it was as I expected." I sat down, waiting for him to question me.

"Think you're out of the woods?"

"I believe so. What reason would I have had to kill that knockout girl?"

"Understood. But now, let's get back to the main topic of conversation. It's the question the police continue to ask again and again. Why did Roberta Simms walk into your meadow to die?"

"I can answer half of this question. I believe Roberta came to my neighborhood to find me. She wasn't in love with me, but she did occasionally like the intimacy. Obviously, she didn't find me that day. From what I've heard about the possible time of death, well, I hadn't seen Roberta anytime within a month of that date."

"How did she arrive in your area? No strange car was ever seen there."

"When I was dating Roberta she didn't have a car. I don't know why. I met her in a mall and drove her home. Her parents were in Canada at the time. No fooling around with Roberta. She didn't even want to stop for a kiss. I think we overdid it a little that night."

"Someone had to bring her to your place the day she died. Any ideas?"

"As I told you the other evening on my cell, I agree with Kim. She swore she saw Roberta climb into police cruisers twice. Kim's always on that street, either on a scooter or cross-country skis."

"What are your plans for this young girl?"

"Probably going to be her guardian angel for a while. Something like that. I sort of like her, though occasionally she's a pain in the butt. By the way, Detective Wonderlich told me this morning he doesn't plan to question her again."

"I'm not at all certain that's wise. I told you the other evening she and Lorna had a big fight when Kim was 11."

"For what reason?"

"Kim wanted a real gun, and Lorna said no."

"I find this hard to believe. Who in hell would give Kim a real gun at the age of 11? Lorna was right on the mark."

"Well, maybe, but listen, you piss this Kim off, she'll stick an ice pick in your throat!"

I laughed out loud. "I'd sooner believe she'd start kissing me to death! Forget about Kim. But remember, Roberta came to the neighborhood to find me. I just don't know why she wandered into that snow covered field."

"How's the search for the Russian coming along? Is he still a suspect? I heard he's broke on his butt and working here in Denver."

"I turned everything over to the police this morning. Between teaching Kim and keeping up with my university courses, I'm literally up to my ears."

Zuckermann lunged at me then, startling me. "Give me a quick answer!" he yelled. "Who killed her?"

"Stipanovitch, or one of the policemen. That's all I have. Without some kind of break in the case, it will never be solved."

Zuckermann was shaking his head wistfully. "That little street, the little hill, the hundreds of yards of grass and weeds, It's an unlikely place for a beautiful young girl to die."

"I sometimes remember an old saying from England. 'The man just ruined that girl! Yes, ruined her!' I believe this happened to Roberta. Someone ruined her. I sat down beside her in the mall holding a half cup of hot chocolate. I asked her if she'd like a cup. 'No,' she answered, 'get me out of here. Take me home. My parents are in Canada.' There you have it."

"Why your success rate with girls?"

I laughed. "That's easy. I'm on the side of the angels. Everybody knows it." I stood, offered my hand, and then slipped out the main door. I glanced toward the blonde behind the desk, sort of caught my breath, and then got out of there!

Two days later I walked up to Kim's house for her history lesson only to find she was not there. When I spoke with Lorna Worthington I found Kim had not yet come home from school. "She might have stopped off with some friend," Lorna suggested. I told her there was no problem, that I would be back tomorrow afternoon.

As I walked down the hill I figured I'd grab my Ford keys from my house and then cruise around the neighborhood for a minute or two. If I didn't see Kim soon I'd drive on to the university library and work for a couple of hours. I'm continuing with my paper dealing with Hawthorne's *The Scarlet Letter*.

I drove along every road in the neighborhood and saw no

young girl walking along. Leave it, I told myself. Kim is 13. She should be able to find her way home, for God's sake. I headed for the university. Once in the library, I took my time pulling eight books on Hawthorne from the shelves and checked them out. It was now nearing dusk. I took the books and walked outside to my car and placed the books in my back seat.

I hesitated for a moment before driving home. Actually, I believe this was the first time Kim had missed our lesson. I thought back to a few months ago, when I first met her, when she was running loose on the streets. Could she possibly have reverted back to her old habits? I recalled the one evening when we met Paul Stipanovitch in the library. As we walked outside to the car later I asked her how she was enjoying our evening out.

"Not quite as interesting as roaming around on my own," she said.

I looked out at the darkening streets of Denver. I should be heading home to work on my term paper, but somehow I'm not quite ready to do this. I just drove around a little. I went down University to Belleview, turned left to Highway 25, headed north to Hampton, and then drove west back to my small home.

I parked my car in front of my house and sat there. I stared at the large fields across the road where Kim had found Roberta's body. She couldn't have gone there. There was no reason to walk through there again, and she had promised not to do it. I continued gazing at the fields. I realized I was allowing my emotions to get the better of me.

Finally I took my books from the back seat and carried them into my house. I forced myself to begin working on my Hawthorne paper. I had trouble focusing. Still, I pressed on for nearly an hour, though not making much progress.

I walked into my living room and looked out my picture window into the darkness. It is, of course, the same window the postman glanced into while walking by, when he had seen Kim and me kissing, and turned us over to Officer Cramer, who had actually given us good advice that day.

I was disgusted with myself because of my concerns. I decided, either I would call the Worthington home, probably making myself look foolish, or grab my big light from the garage and search the entire area of 'the fields' right now in the darkness. This is turning into a horror story. Every day since Kim had discovered Roberta's body I have stared into those fields and shuddered slightly. Now I'm considering going into them at night! I reached for my cell phone.

"Mrs. Worthington, this is Michael, have you heard from Kim yet?" After several seconds I got a small "no."

"All right now, how long before your husband is home?"

"Perhaps half an hour. I'm very worried." Her voice seemed far away.

"Try and stay calm. I'm going to look around a little."

I took a deep breath and then went into my garage for the big light. There was no sense in waiting.

The tall grass was difficult at night. Still, I adjusted. And 200 yards were a mere trifling. Of course, I planned to be all over this park during the next hour. My nerves are good. Why in hell should I imagine somebody else is stumbling around out here in the night? It's like a cemetery.

My light is strong. I can easily see out 50 feet. Wait, there is something. No, just a large clump of grass. Forward. Once in a while I shined the light to the left and then to the right. I generally kept moving ahead, though. Now I saw something, really something. Yes, a form on the ground. I was proud of myself. I didn't even hesitate. A few seconds later I was kneeling over a horribly brutalized Kim. I thought she was dead.

There were no houses in sight. I grabbed for my cell and tried several numbers without success. The damned battery must be getting weak. I was on my knees, gently feeling Kim's left wrist for a pulse. I can't get any. I softly felt the area around her throat. I've heard there was sometimes a pulse there. If there is one, it is faint. I felt her tiny arms and believe they were both broken. I could tell nothing about her legs. Her eyes were closed. Did this mean she was alive? I grabbed my cell again but it was completely dead now.

Should I carry her out? But how many times have I heard people caution: "Do not move the injured." I don't give a damn. I'm not waiting any longer. The light has a loop on it. I hooked it around my left little finger, then in clumsy fashion I picked Kim up. Even before I moved forward I was crying.

Although she must be five-feet-seven, she was so light I can't think she measured a hundred pounds. The light dangling from my finger jiggled strangely. I believe I've seen Kim's chest move and I continued to hope. Right now her life was more important to me than my own. The tears reached my chin but I don't care. I moved forward as best I could, hoping against hope I wouldn't fall.

I had reached the first 100 yards. I saw a car with bright lights coming from the left along the road. This person was likely to notice my own wobbly light. Yes, the car was slowing down. I believe it is a large Mercedes. I proceeded 'steady as she goes.' The car had stopped. Forty yards to go; I was still easily carrying Kim in my arms, though my footing was now unsteady.

The man in the car was Kim's father coming home. As soon as I heard his voice I called out, "I have Kim. She's been badly injured. We need to get her to a hospital as soon as possible."

He ran forward and took the light. A few seconds later we gently lifted Kim into the large back seat. I lay on the floorboards and held her hand.

"Drive the car," I begged. "We'll talk later."

"Right," he said emphatically. "My God, will it never end?"

Kim slowly opened her eyes and then closed them again.

Later I felt her squeeze my hand. After that I began crying like a baby. I just couldn't help it!

In the hospital they operated on Kim for more than four hours. Stan Worthington and I sat around totally in shock, and mostly silent. We had no idea why Kim had gone into the fields, nor can I explain why I went in to look for her there. Lorna Worthington joined us after a while and the three of us sat around together, mostly still numb with shock.

At last I saw another friendly face, Detective Wilson Cramer, who immediately waved me over and asked me to take a chair. He told me he had been called in by the department an hour ago.

"Just a few questions," he said. "I know you're probably frantic with worry."

"I'm just praying she makes it. When I first found her I thought she was dead."

"You saved her life, you know. But what made you go back into those fields?"

"We have a history lesson almost every day after school. When I went to her house I found Kim hadn't come home yet. I told Mrs. Worthington that there was no problem, that we could have our next lesson tomorrow afternoon. I walked back down the hill to my house, took my car keys and, as an afterthought, drove around for a couple of minutes, thinking I might see Kim coming home. I obviously had no luck. I had work to do at the university library and so I drove there, though still feeling somewhat restless."

"Because of the murder of Roberta Simms?"

"Yes. I've never been comfortable looking at those fields since Roberta's death. I checked some books out of the library and took them out to my car. Then I just sat there, thinking."

"How much time had elapsed since you left Kim's home?"

"Perhaps just over two hours. Please understand, I had absolutely no reason to be concerned yet. For all I knew, Kim was already safe at home."

Cramer had been writing on his pad. "So following this, you drove back to your house with your books."

I shook my head. "Not quite. I just drove around. I went down University to Belleview, turned left to Highway 25, took it north to Hampton, and then wound my way back west to my house. I parked my car, turned off the motor, and stared into the fields. I sat there for at least 10 minutes. By then it was totally dark. Eventually I took my books inside and began working on my English term paper at my kitchen table."

I saw a physician walking toward Mr. and Mrs. Worthington. "Just a minute, Detective. I'll be right back." I quickly walked across the room, but paused a couple of steps back from the others. The physician had at least some good news.

"Your daughter has made it through the operation," he said. "She's still critical, of course. She may be in intensive care for several days." He glanced back at me. "Are you the young man who carried her out to safety?"

I nodded. "I couldn't leave her there. I thought she was dying."

"You probably saved her life. Usually, though, it's not advisable to move the injured party. This time it worked okay." I nodded again and raised my hand in agreement. I walked back to Cramer.

"She's holding her own," I told the detective.

"Kids are tough." He gave me a smile, but then paused for a few seconds. "It seems incredible that you were somehow persuaded to go into those damned fields. You had no real reason, did you? It must have been nerve racking."

"It didn't happen all at once. It became more and more difficult to concentrate on my term paper as the evening progressed. Although I hadn't planned to call the Worthington family again, little by little I realized I would need to do exactly that. It was as though Roberta's murder had somehow been reawakened in my mind. I knew I wouldn't be able to sleep unless I did something, so I picked up my cell. As soon as I heard Kim was still missing, I grabbed my large flashlight from the garage and followed the same path Kim, the police and I had taken to find Roberta's body. I found Kim lying less than five feet away from where Roberta had been."

"We have a killer loose in your fields," Cramer said.

"I know, and I seriously doubt you'll ever solve this case unless a huge break comes along. It's becoming a horror story. That's what I thought earlier last night." I paused. "Anything else?"

"Nothing right now. Good luck with your young friend." We shook hands and I walked back over to the Worthingtons.

The three of us discussed our options. Although it was obvious there was nothing any of us could do for Kim at this late hour, we continued going over every aspect of the horrible attack from all angles. With the operation over and Kim bearing up as best as could be expected, I realized I was pretty much out of the picture in terms of helping. Not being an actual member of the family, even if I remained here until morning light, no one was going to give me any additional information about Kim, and I would certainly not be able to see her.

I urged the Worthingtons to follow my example and go home and get some rest. We could take up the cause again tomorrow. Kim's mother had one final question for me, however. I remembered now that she had arrived at the hospital later and hadn't heard all of our earlier discussion. She naturally wanted to know what had caused me to go into the fields after dark.

"There was no reason," I told her. "Except, once I called you, and discovered that Kim was not yet home, I was just drawn into those fields. I didn't want to go. I had to go. And thank God I did. I honestly don't believe Kim could have made it through the night." The Worthingtons nodded in agreement.

"Did I really believe Kim was lying there helpless? No, I did not. But I was affected by the death of Roberta earlier and also, I had no other place to look. I would not have been able to sleep anyway had I not searched those fields."

"I believe I'll stay here for a while," Kim's father said abruptly. "Michael will need a ride, of course."

"I have no classes tomorrow so I should be back here early. I'll no doubt meet the two of you at some time or other." Lorna Worthington and I walked out to her car.

Had I known the kind of driver she was I doubt I would have gotten into the car at all. After two blocks I begged her to pull over and let me take the wheel. She was shaking so badly she gladly followed my advice. I was hoping she could make it around the car without fainting. After we had traded places I drove steadily back toward our own neighborhood.

"I'll drive you directly up to your house," I said later. "The walk down the hill will do me good."

"You'll be passing directly by the fields," she said.

"It's getting on toward morning. I'm not worried about it." Several minutes later we drove up and parked on the east side of the large home.

"How could this have happened?" she asked me. I knew she probably wanted to talk for a minute or two.

"The police were baffled earlier with the murder of Roberta Simms. I doubt if they have the slightest idea yet who attacked Kim." I glanced over at her. "Do you have any kind of medicine to take, to try and get at least a little sleep? Excuse me, but you're a nervous wreck. Tomorrow the police may be dropping by. You should prepare for this visit."

"I saw you talking with someone earlier. Was he a detective?"

"Yes. I knew him from before because of the death of Roberta. He wanted as much information as possible about the reason I went into the fields. That was his major concern. It seemed to him as though I had already known where Kim was. Actually, what really happened was a combination of nervousness and stupidity. We just happened to luck out."

"Kim has been much better behaved since she met you. Of course, she's awfully young to be your student."

"I understand. I'm five years her senior. Of course, she'll soon meet many other young men. And let's remember, 13-year-old girls are notably unpredictable."

"At least her studies continue to improve."

"Absolutely, and I'm pleased about that." We were both silent for a moment. "I have a question," I said finally. "It concerned something that happened when Kim was 11."

"Who told you about this?"

"Lawyer Zuckermann. Did Kim really argue about buying a gun?"

Rather than answer me directly, she touched the left side of her neck. "She poked me with a very large fork. I told you once before, I can't control her."

I almost began smiling, but I held back. "You're a grown woman. Kim's sort of a tall skinny kid. Surely, there must have been ways. My God, who do you imagine her to be? Lizzie Borden?"

She paused again. "I can't control her," she said quietly.

"We talk about the problems Kim causes, yet here she is, wrapped up like a mummy in a hospital. I'll bet when I'm finally able to peak in her room her face will still be completely bandaged. Did you know when I carried her the 200 yards out to the road I was crying so hard the tears were running off my chin. I'm fond of Kim." I laughed. "Of course, not really like a girlfriend. I hope Kim understands the difference."

"You are far better than me keeping her under control. You're already like a teacher, even at your young age."

"That's because I started early. I began reading small books when I was four. I've always been fascinated by language. History too, of course. I've also had three years of German, though no one ever hears me speak it." I paused. "Now what else should I know about Kim? What else has she done?"

"She's thrown herself against us more than once. I hate to keep speaking negatively about her when she's hurt so badly now, but she has been a problem for us. She once struck my husband in the head with a golf club. He was out cold for a few seconds."

I clamped my mouth tight, trying not to grin, although it's really not funny. "Tell me honestly, do you ever give Kim hugs?"

Total silence. For a few seconds I was afraid she was never going to answer me. Finally in a whispered voice, she said: "I'd be afraid she would bite me."

At first I thought she was making a joke, but I soon saw she was serious. I'm convinced something is wrong with Lorna Worthington. She speaks softly with little variance in pitch. Also, not only is she spectacularly beautiful, I believe what Kim told me—23 years old!

"Have you ever had her speak with a psychologist?" I asked.

"Once. She threw such a fit we never tried it again." Suddenly Lorna took my hand and squeezed it softly. Considering the circumstances I let her hold it.

"Let me understand something. Kim's been out of control, even violent, and then for a time was running away from home late at night with no one putting a stop to it. Excuse me, but much of this is difficult for me to understand."

"We were too weak," she said.

"Perhaps that explains everything," I said finally. "You were too weak." I took my hand away gently. "And so, let's get this car into the garage. Don't forget to close up. You're distraught. Don't worry about Kim. She's really banged up, but I'm convinced she's going to make it. I'll probably see you again tomorrow in the hospital. I'll try and be there early."

I walked down the hill with my eyes naturally sometimes fixed on 'the fields.' Who had attacked these two girls? I have no better idea than the police. Again, as I told Detective Cramer, I'm convinced this case will never be solved without some kind of major breakthrough.

Just before 8:00 the next morning I heard someone pounding on my front door. It was a police officer I had never seen before. Looking past him into 'the fields' I saw other officers walking through the tall grass. I also noticed three patrol cars parked across the street, heading up the hill toward Kim's house."

"Hello," the officer at my door said. "How about I come in and ask a few questions? I'm Officer Genavissie, head man on this case."

"No problem." I led him into my living room.

"You are Michael Sheppard, I believe," he said. "The young man who found the Worthington girl over there." He glanced out my picture window. "What made you decide to go into those fields in the night?"

"I'm not certain I can explain it. I thought about a lot of things last evening before I became involved. I had originally planned to write an English term paper. That's it on the kitchen table back there around the corner."

He immediately walked back to check it. This officer appeared dead serious, I thought, and not particularly friendly.

"Why so many books?" he asked when he returned. "They

all seem to be about that 'scarlet letter' person from way back when.'"

"I guess that's right. I didn't get very far with the paper last night." I noticed Genavissie had been taking copious notes.

"Talk to me a little about your relationship with the Worthington girl. That might be helpful."

"Of course." I took a deep breath. "As you probably know, Kim lives four houses up the hill on the left. She's 13 years old and I've known her since moving here last August."

"Probably has a crush on you?"

"Maybe. She's an extremely bright kid who does well in school."

"And you're a student at the university?"

"Yes, I'm a freshman there."

"So, I guess she's your girlfriend."

I smiled. "She's a little too young for me. I'm 18. She's just a neighborhood kid I happen to know."

"Well, I certainly agree, the girl is too young for you. Anyway, why don't you just explain your relationship with the Worthington family."

"I don't know exactly what you want."

"How many times has the young girl been here in this house, for example?"

"Twice. The second time was just after she found the body of Roberta Simms over in 'the fields.' We were on the phone reporting this finding to the police."

"What about the first time?"

"I think perhaps you know."

"Why don't you answer my question?"

"It was her 13th birthday. I gave her a three-second kiss."

"On the mouth?"

"Yes. Our postman saw us kissing through that window there and turned us in. An important case. I feel it is imperative to protect young girls from getting kissed too much!"

"Don't fool with me, young man. It annoys me. And so now you're playing the hero. Finding this Kim over in 'the fields' and carrying her out to the road in the dark. But I can think of another interesting scenario. Let's say the two of you were fooling around. Maybe the girl changed her mind. Somebody nearly killed her, and you can't give me a reason why you went back into those fields. It's suspicious."

"I carried Kim out to her father."

"We'll soon be questioning the young girl. She'll tell us what happened before this."

"She will? Better be cautious here, officer. She may tell you to go fuck yourself! Kim is a 'spitfire' who likes all the kisses she can get!"

Genavissie stood up in a huff! "Keep your mouth going, you'll end up in jail!" He walked toward the front door, but paused at the corner, which led to the kitchen. Who do you have for a lawyer, young student-type?"

"Ben Zuckermann, I said. "Same lawyer Kim has."

"Son of a bitch!" I heard him say while walking away.

Leaving my house for the hospital I glanced across the road past the three police cruisers and into the fields where the officers were still milling around. I was not happy with my performance with Genavissie. My God, I've portrayed Kim as a kind of freak, out of control, and myself as an enabler. I need to start watching myself. Actually, Kim and I haven't shared even five kisses in all the months I've known her.

When I arrived at the hospital I found Lorna Worthington sitting in the main lobby with additional news. "No police have been allowed in Kim's room yet, and she is at least holding her own." She continued. "My husband, however, is ready to break a major hospital rule. He would like for you to go to room 226 immediately and visit briefly with Kim. He's convinced your visit would be a major psychological boost for her. You should go now. The police have been here looking for you. Please go before they find you."

I was in the elevator within seconds. I had noted Lorna was more under control this morning.

Outside room 226 Stan Worthington was pacing the hall. "My God, what happened? We've been frantic here!"

"The police grabbed me at my house before I could leave. How is she?"

"No worse, thank God. We need you in that room now, though. You will be a big help to her. She can't lift her arms. Perhaps you could touch her right hand. Stay only for a few seconds. If the police find you here, they'll demand entrance themselves. They've been here before, right in this hallway."

When I saw Kim I was horrified. No wonder her father was beside himself. Almost her entire face was bandaged. I walked quietly to her bed. I followed my instructions and gently touched her right hand.

"Michael?" When she spoke the entire bandage moved. Her voice was so soft I scarcely recognized it.

"I'm here, Kim." There was a long pause.

"I live for you, Michael" I squeezed her hand.

I knew I had to leave. I stood up and stepped away.

"Michael?" I paused and leaned down again. "All is fair in love and war." I imagined her giving me a smile. At that moment I knew she was going to make it.

"Run for it," her father told me as I left the room. "We'll talk later."

Detective Cramer, however, met me a few feet from the elevator. "We'll need to visit the station," he told me. "They'll probably keep you there for a while. Probably until Genavissie is convinced you had a real reason for exploring those fields in the dark of night.

I'm sorry." We left the hospital in a patrol car.

On the way to the station Cramer filled me in on Genavissie's rational for the case dealing with the attack on Kim. "It happened long ago, but once you've heard the story I think you'll understand his feelings. His younger sister was 14 years old at the time. She was seduced by another officer on the force. Genavissie actually shot him later, though only in the right shoulder. Still, it put a crimp in his career."

"I'm glad you told me this. It does help me understand his attitude."

"Although I will never admit saying this, it is what I believe. This is all a fake run dealing more with the past than any case dealing with present-day violence. You are being held in the station for a while simply because you are 18, five years older than Kim."

"Doesn't seem very fair. I have a young kid I care about, bandaged up like a mummy, and perhaps still near death, lying in a hospital which I'm not going to be able to visit for the duration. Good God!"

"Don't mention the kid too much around the station if you please. In our present society 'love and caring' are sometimes dirty words."

"In my case 'caring' with Kim meant three or four kisses over many months, and that's it."

"Still and all."

"If you could, please enlighten me as to what I'm to expect at the station. A room, a cell, torture, a firing squad?"

"Don't kid around." Cramer paused. "You'll probably get a room. There will be questions of course. Mostly the same question. What made you decide to go into 'the fields' at night? It's a question many are asking."

"Should I be calling Zuckermann?"

He sighed. "It all depends on Kim. As soon as she gets better she'll be demanding your release. She'll naturally call in her father and Zuckermann, and they'll start raising hell all over the place," He laughed. "Remember, Kim is only a year younger than Joan of Ark. She's tough! Of course, once she gives testimony to the police about the attack, surely nothing will matter much any longer. She will have given a good description of the real criminal who attacked her. And let's remember, Genavisse is running a bluff here. He doesn't really believe you harmed your young friend. After all, you're the one who carried her to the street to safety. Her own father witnessed this."

"The main danger for you now will be your own emotions. Don't forget, it won't be Wonderlich or me in that room with you. The others are going to lean hard. It's their job. They'll hope you lose control. Don't refer to Kim as a 'spitfire.' Don't become a 'hotshot' yourself. It's a simple waiting game now. Well, here we are." We pulled up by the side of the station.

Walking inside we found Wonderlich standing near the room I had visited once before. He was shaking his head. "A setback," he told us. "The young lady, Kim, has elapsed into a coma. The physicians expect her to regain consciousness soon, but now everything is in limbo." He glanced at me. "I'm sorry, but we'll need to take your cell phone. Would you like us to bring one of our phones into this room for you? You could use it to make a couple of calls if you wish."

I nodded. "Thank you both very much." Within two minutes a female officer brought me a phone. Well, good, my cell was worthless anyway. I had already pulled the number of Zuckermann's law office from my billfold. I need out of this goddamned place. And quick! I assumed the lady who answered the phone was the blonde secretary I've already met.

"Hello. I'm Michael Sheppard. I'm in the police station. I need to speak with Ben Zuckermann as soon as possible." There was a hesitation.

"I'm sorry. Mr. Zuckermann is unavailable and may be for

some time."

"What's wrong? Is he ill?" These questions were asked in a voice slightly higher than usual.

More hesitation. Did I hear soft laughter in the background?

"Actually, he's busy screwing his blonde secretary in Barbados at present. I'm his wife. I'm in the process of filing for divorce. Goodbye." I heard a click.

The young female officer entered the room and reached for the phone. I handed it to her and gave her a smile. "If you could pass along a message," I said. "I'm ready to be questioned at any time." She nodded and left my room, the one with the light green paint, which might be designed to force the guilty into submission.

From hero to suspect, I thought, in less than 24 hours. Meanwhile, I don't have the slightest idea about Kim's condition. Leaving me alone in this room must be part of Genavisse's revenge. Twenty minutes passed, then 40.

I took a deep breath. My parents were out of touch in Hawaii, my ex-lawyer was making out with his blonde secretary in Barbados, the Worthingtons were frightened out of their wits near room 226 in the hospital, and the light green paint continued closing in on me tighter and tighter with every passing moment.

Well, young student-type, you want to start bawling into your arms on the table, or become a man and suck it up? Your name means archangel. By now I'm almost snarling. By God, let's suck it up!

After more than an hour I was convinced no one was interested in questioning me. In order to keep my sanity I needed to concentrate on something else. I thought of my university classes, which recently I'd been forced to ignore. I thought about Kim naturally, and another girl, now deceased, who I had not loved, but who I would admit to anyone who asked, had more to do with my growing up than any other person in the world. It's probably because of all the violence I have witnessed recently that I thought again of Roberta.

I recalled the evening we first met, when she asked me to drive her to an empty house while her parents were on vacation. It was a strange experience. And what was it about the kisses? That, I was never able to understand. It became evident to me that evening that Roberta had little use for affection, and preferred to advance to sex immediately. I laughed. And as for holding hands and the like? Well, she would just as soon spit in your eye.

It was true that first night when we were together in her bedroom, she kissed me while climaxing, but that was more like an attack! She would yank my head down, bruise my mouth, and come close to knocking out teeth. A crazy kind of girl. I paused, shaking my head. And I have wished a hundred times since that I could have somehow saved her.

There was no clock in the room with the light green paint, and they had taken away my worthless cell. I'm just guessing now, but I believe I must have been in this room for nearly two hours. God, I suddenly realized I hadn't visited a bathroom since being questioned by Genavisse earlier this morning in my house. I needed a men's room.

Of course, I already know the young police officer at the front desk, the same one who had handed me a phone, and then taken it away later. I'll bet she will be happy to direct me to a men's room. I stepped out of my prison home and walked to her desk. Not only did she point out the way, she gave me a big bright smile as well. I'll bet if women were running this goddamned planet they would never let the likes of me near a police station. They would instead take me home and cuddle me forever, and I would give them all the poetry they could stand.

When I returned in about five minutes, the young officer left her desk and walked with me back to my dungeon. She had her left hand on my shoulder. God, I thought, maybe she planned to cuddle me right here in the station. I placed my right hand firmly around her waist, just as I had with Roberta when we were strolling along a path in the mountains. I'm hoping against hope. Coming to my door, though, she held up a big key and laughed at me.

"Don't want me to escape, huh," I said, leering a little. She opened the door. Then I heard the sound of a 'click.'"

Twenty more minutes passed and I have yet to see a soul for the questioning session. Finally, I heard Wonderlich's voice outside my door. He was speaking with the young female officer I had already seen three times before. She naturally had to unlock my door. She waved to me and returned to her desk, while Wonderlich walked toward me carrying a can of Coke. He handed it to me.

"They aren't coming," he said. "You've waited long enough. Detective Cramer has a car outside to take you back to the hospital. If you get any more news about the attack on your young friend, please call me. We're making no progress on either of these cases." We shook hands and once again I exited the station.

In the hospital I found no one in the lobby I knew and so I took the elevator up to the second floor and walked down to 226. Stan Worthington was sitting in a chair near Kim's room, which was closed. I raised my hand in greeting and pulled a second chair up a few feet away. "Is Kim still in a coma?" I asked softly.

"Actually, it's a medically-induced coma," he said. "They can bring her out of it whenever they choose. She was simply too restless this morning. It was shortly after you left that they made the decision."

"And where might Mrs. Worthington be? I didn't see her down in the lobby."

"Oh, she returned home today." He smiled. "Seems she's having one of her nervous encounters. I imagine she's already back in bed."

I nodded and paused for a moment. "I've had a long conversation with Detective Wilson Cramer. He drove me to the station in his patrol car. Detective Genavisse, who questioned me earlier this morning, was the gentleman who demanded I be taken in for additional questioning. I sat there in a room alone for just short of three hours. No one came to ask me anything. I believe the entire exercise was simply harassment on Genavisse's part. I know one thing. After talking with Cramer and Wonderlich, I found their department has made little or no progress with either Roberta's murder or the attack on Kim. I guess I'm not surprised."

After a time Kim's father began smiling. "Did you attempt to call lawyer Zuckermann while you were in captivity?"

"Oh, yes, I actually spoke with his wife. She's holding down the fort now, looking forward to when the big man returns from Barbados, so she can zap him." I grinned. "She made it clear she knows he took his blonde secretary along. She's already filing for divorce."

"Yes, all true unfortunately. Looks like we've lost our lawyer friend for a while."

I glanced at Kim's closed door. "Are they checking on Kim regularly?"

"At least every 10 or 15 minutes. They should be coming along soon. They won't let you in the room, though. Ah, I think I see two of them coming now."

"Just trying to peek in?" the accompanying nurse asked, smiling.

I nodded. Boy, Stan Worthington was right. The door closed immediately behind the health care couple. I did notice that Kim was bandaged exactly as she had been earlier this morning. Of course, I wouldn't have expected it to be otherwise.

When Kim's father and I were alone again sitting in the hallway, I decided to ask him a couple of questions about his wife. Probably I should have done this long ago. "Something has been bothering me," I said. "As you may know, I drove your wife's BMW home last night. She was too nervous to drive herself." He nodded.

"During the trip we spoke about Kim. I brought up something Mr. Zuckermann had told me about an argument Kim had with your wife when she was 11. It concerned the purchase of a gun, not the toy fake Luger, but a real gun. Is this true?"

"First of all, what did Kim tell you about the little toy gun, which you referred to as a fake Luger?"

"I can still remember. It was the first day we met. She told me she had purchased a real Luger from a drunk near the mall, and that he had died soon afterward near a large garbage container."

"Ah, a drunk on the street." He laughed. "Actually, I purchased the toy gun for Kim. I did it soon after the argument you referred to. And as for the argument itself, well, I certainly remember that. And yes, it concerned the purchase of a weapon. But surely you know by now, no one in his right mind was going to give Kim a real weapon. Hell, if she got into a bad mood, she might start blasting dogs, cats and lord, even postmen. I'm sort of joking, of course."

"So you're saying the report was accurate, up to a point."

"What else did my wife tell you?"

I hesitated at first, but decided to press on. "By then we were parked on the east side of your home. Your wife placed the forefinger of her left hand on her neck. She told me the wound occurred when Kim stuck a fork in her."

Stan laughed. "Did the wound appear to come from a fork of some kind?"

"No, it did not. I could believe it came from an ice pick, or something similar."

Stan laughed again. "The wound was from a BB. It happened when my wife was 12 years old. A neighbor boy accidently shot her in the neck. It had nothing to do with Kim."

"But what did Kim do during the argument?"

"Probably screamed around a little. The only reason she doesn't scream around you is she's in love with you and wants to appear mature. But let's remember one important fact here. The only reason Kim wanted a weapon was because she was running wild into the city at night. Since she isn't doing this any longer, she doesn't need a gun for protection."

"Another question, this one more serious. Did Kim ever knock you out by striking you with a golf club?"

"No. If I ever saw Kim coming at me with a golf club, I would simply take it away from her. You'll remember, however, that I've never condoned corporal punishment."

I paused for a moment. The health care duo was coming out of Kim's room. They stopped directly in front of Stan Worthington and gave him a brief report. The physician in charge was speaking. "There is little change," he began, "which is not necessarily bad. We're monitoring your daughter carefully. She's a strong, healthy young lady. I'm optimistic." He shook hands with Stan and the physician and his nurse walked away.

I returned to the former topic of conversation. "After speaking with your wife in the middle of the night, and noticing she was a total nervous wreck, I wondered if perhaps it might not have been better if Kim, at a younger age, had had her little butt spanked a few times."

He smiled. "Well, everyone should make their own decisions about this. Of course, as I've told you, I'm against corporal punishment."

"The phrase Mrs. Worthington repeated more than once in her car was, 'I can't control her.' Another phrase that stuck with me was, I don't ever hug Kim because I'm afraid."

"Did she say what she was afraid of?"

"Well, yes. It was about being bitten."

"Good God!" He was chuckling again now. "Tell me, when you heard about Kim knocking me out, didn't you almost begin laughing?"

"No doubt about it."

"Right. Now let's speak a little truth here." He paused again. "Let's both admit that my wife is a beautiful woman."

"I totally agree."

"Now let's examine a scenario. Let's say that one day, for whatever reason, you are alone with my wife in our large kitchen. Perhaps she had attempted to make coffee for you. God forbid! Let's pretend that things have not gone well for my wife on this particular day. She is, as you stated before, a nervous wreck. Her face is pale and her hands are shaking a little. Surely, you are thinking, a platonic hug would help, perhaps a little stroking of the upper back. Now I've often noticed that you're a tall, physically strong young man. Well, you would need to be. With the platonic hug, what you would suddenly have on your hands is Raggedy Ann."

"Raggedy Ann?"

"Yes. A totally collapsed woman. A rag doll. You would have to hold her up. By the way, how was the coffee she made those many months ago when you were there after Kim hit you on the head with the baseball?"

"I can't remember. I had other things on my mind."

"What was your opinion of my wife that day? Oh, come on. We might as well be honest here."

I gazed at him seriously. "Okay, I thought she was a hippie type. She was calling me 'Dude' and gave me slow, exaggerated hand gestures and said she couldn't control her daughter. After I told her that Kim needed more young friends, she told me to forget it, that I should just enjoy my young ward."

"Tell me, why do you think my wife was so concerned about our daughter?"

"I am not certain. I was tempted at first to think it was fear."

"Again, what would she have been afraid of? You surely know, the only reason Kim hit you in the head that day was jealously. I also heard what she told you this morning," he said, pointing to her room.

"You mean, 'all is fair in love and war'?"

"Exactly. She's not going to allow her own boyfriend to escape." He laughed, but then continued in a more serious vein. "Though I consider myself to be a kind, caring husband, and I love my wife very much, it doesn't seem to matter at all. You see, regardless of how I approach my spouse, the result is the same." He glanced over at me. "I always find a beautiful, limp Raggedy Ann in my bed. My wife has been taking far too many pills over the past several years. I fear she is addicted."

Leaving the hospital, my mind filled with clutter, I drove directly to a large gun shop where I purchased a Glock 9mm without any problem. I was sick of staring over at 'the fields,' realizing I had no protection. I don't plan to carry the Glock in the university, though I'm certain it will often be in my car or my house.

Because Stan Worthington was paying me well to visit Kim, I do this though usually I'm just hanging around the hall and can't see his daughter anyway. Today will probably be the same.

This morning I was in the university for the first time in three days and felt good about it. There had been no pop quizzes in any of my classes, which was welcome news. After briefly visiting Kim this afternoon, by 7:00 I planned to be working at home on my Hawthorne paper. It was due in six days. Entering the hospital, I found that room 226 was still closed to me. I wasn't surprised.

After 20 minutes I grew tired of sitting and began pacing the hallway for some exercise. I'd been at this for perhaps 10 minutes when I saw a doctor, a nurse and Detective Wonderlich coming down the hall toward me. Kim must be out of her coma, I thought. Otherwise Wonderlich wouldn't be here. When the Detective saw me standing there he nudged the physician's arm. I'm certain he's asking if I can accompany him into Kim's room because I'm so well acquainted with her.

"Following our examination, the two of you can go in for five minutes," the physician said, smiling. "My nurse, Ms. Hardgrave, will remain here and make certain you stick to the allotted time. The health care duo slipped into Kim's room and the door closed behind them.

Wonderlich and I shook hands. I asked him if he had his questions for Kim lined up.

"We need a physical description of the attacker," he told me. "Also, anything he might have said and whether she thinks she might have seen him before."

"Are you certain the attacker was a man?" I asked.

"How can I know for sure? Your friend inside that room should be able to enlighten us."

"Yesterday the doctors medically induced Kim into a coma. I didn't know they had brought her out of it until I saw the three of you coming down the hall."

Wonderlich was shaking his head. "Unless she somehow recognized the person in that field, I can't think this interview will amount to much."

"I agree with you, but we have to start some place."

The nurse and the physician exited Kim's room and the doctor left us at once, heading down the hall toward the elevator. Nurse Hardgrave remained with us and, after a few seconds she, Wonderlich and myself entered Kim's room.

"Kimo," I said. "Detective Wonderlich has a few questions regarding the afternoon you were attacked."

Kim looked up at Wonderlich. She remembered him from Zuckermann's office.

The detective nodded to her. "First of all, can you give us a description of the person who attacked you?"

"The attacker was almost as tall as Michael, but with a noticeable paunch. I don't believe I'd seen the person before, though I could be wrong. You see, it all happened so fast. The person was strong. Otherwise, I would have put up more of a fight."

"Did the man say anything?"

"No, he didn't. Though I'm not convinced this was a man. The person wore a stocking cap. Had Roberta Simms not been dead, I could have thought it might have been her. Except, of course, for the paunch, which could have been faked."

"Can you tell us what you were doing in 'the fields' that afternoon?"

"No, I can't. I simply don't remember going there. I had promised Michael never to go near 'the fields' again. As I think back, it was as though I had been transported into that place by some kind of strange force."

The detective was scratching his head. "Is there anything else you want to tell us?"

Kim paused. Finally, smiling, she gave me a wink. "Visit me quick!" she said.

Again, out in the hall, Wonderlich expressed his exasperation. Damned near worthless," he said. "And that business about being transported into the fields by another force, and a dead girl attacking her there. When I hear that kind of rubbish I'm ready to go back to considering her a suspect."

"Doesn't quite work though, does it? I mean, you surely can't be thinking Kim brutalized herself that afternoon."

"She gave herself a bloody nose before, just to have an excuse to knock on your front door."

"Kim would have died that night had I not found her. And surely you agree, the person who killed Roberta also attacked Kim."

"But why? Why? There was practically no connection between the two young women. The connection was yourself." He was looking at me seriously.

"You surely can't be thinking I attacked the kid in those fields. Surely not."

"No. No. He paused. "But what do you think you're going to do with her during the next few years? Jesus! Talk about bearing a cross. And have you met the mother yet? Surely you have. A druggy and a fruit cake." He hesitated again. "Well, maybe between the father and yourself you can handle those two frustrated females. I just hope I never have to meet up with your extended family in the future. God Almighty!"

I laughed. "Oh sometimes people change, though I'll admit I have little hope for the mother."

"Yeah, with that one we'd need a reincarnation of Sigmund Freud. God, I have to stop talking like this. I keep forgetting how young you are."

"Doesn't matter. I'd never repeat your words, Detective. Not even to the 'spitfire' in that room over there."

That evening while working on my large term paper, I received a phone call from Stan Worthington requesting that I spend an hour with Kim the next afternoon, reminding me to include the extra time on my next bill. He also mentioned that his daughter should remain relatively quiet during the hour; though, of course, she could say a few words once in a while. I told him there would be no problem visiting Kim. I returned to my Hawthorne paper, though still wondering what in hell I was going to talk about tomorrow afternoon. I guess for once, I'd just wing it.

On the way to the hospital the next day I decided to tell Kim a story about the only time I'd been spanked in school, followed by an exciting tale about my young girlfriend who led me into a deep dark forest that same day with a little dictionary taped to her left wrist.

I knocked softly on 226 and entered Kim's room. "Because the powers that be still don't want you talking much, today we will have a story about the one and only time I was spanked in school."

"You were spanked? In school?"

"Yes. 4th grade. And please be quiet. The powers that be, you know. It all began with our teacher, Ms. Roundtree, a full-blooded Cherokee Native American, probably 22 years old, who had not the slightest idea about how to control 20 kids in one classroom. It was only because we kids actually wanted to learn that there was any semblance of order at all."

"So Ms. Roundtree had no control? Was that really her name?"

"Shh. Let me talk. Yes, that was her name and she was a complete Twinkie. But also one of the sweetest ladies known to man."

Kim laughed. "But a Twinkie."

"Yes. But we were all white-bread kids, except for one girl from Mexico, so there was really not much of a problem. We kids knew how to run a classroom. The only thing that annoyed me was how some good advice from a principal or superintendent was stretched into pure annoyance by Ms. Roundtree. As I said, the advice itself was good. Simply put, it stated that all students stay on the school grounds during recess. We dare not stray. Now here's the reason I rebelled and eventually got whacked."

"The spanking?"

"Yes. Yes. That's right. You see, every morning Ms. Roundtree opened the day with the same phrase: 'One dare not stray from the reservation.' And then she'd chuckle just a little, pleased I guess that she could imagine all of us fourth graders being on some reservation under her control. Of course, it could have been the chuckle that annoyed me so much. I don't know."

"What did you do?"

"Well, I decided to strike back during morning recess. I strayed from the reservation, hands in my pockets, whistling, feeling I suppose like 'Cool Hand Luke.' Of course I was eventually caught."

"Where?"

"Oh, a few hundred yards toward the town's little main street. I was dragged back to the school at the end of recess."

"You weren't dragged back," Kim interrupted.

"Well, taken back. But now comes the torture business."

"Torture?"

"Yes. But first you must have an idea of where I sat in my classroom. I was right up front, sitting by my girlfriend, Wilhelmina Huff. We were the only students in this row."

"Both fourth graders."

"Yes. By now the entire class had reassembled. We had allowed the Twinkie to take charge again. These were her first words following recess, after taking a deep breath. "One of our tribe has strayed from the reservation," she began.

"She didn't say 'tribe,'" Kim said. "Come on now."

"Well, she might have said 'student.' I don't know. That was a long time ago. I remember she did say, 'There must be ramifications.' I glanced around at some of my buddies. They were chewing on the big 'ram' word. Does this mean Michael's going to be rammed?"

"No," Kim said. "It means he's going to be whacked!"

"Yes. Yes. But now comes the torture business. We'd been discussing Thomas Jefferson and the Louisiana Purchase. Three sentences into this lecture Ms. Roundtree stopped short, folded her hands in front of her chest, and repeated her warning. 'There must be...ramifications...for straying...off the reservation!'"

"Is she chuckling? No, she seems dead serious now. My classmates have been whispering a lot and have pretty much accepted my punishment in their minds."

"Where's the paddle?" Kim asked.

"It's coming," I said. "But Ms. Roundtree needs to lecture us three more times before she gets it. The lectures are of course interspersed with warnings. That is, THERE MUST BE...."

"Stop it, stop it," Kim said. "I've already memorized the warnings. Move on."

"Well, we're already up to the Lewis and Clark Expedition, which meant a fateful moment. Ms. Roundtree had folded her hands in front of her chest again, but now she looked directly at me. Her arms suddenly dropped to her sides. There was dead silence in the classroom. But then, in a dramatic fashion, she finally said..."I SHALL RETURN."

"Are you telling me she jumped back to MacArthur leaving the Philippines on the way to getting the paddle?" (Kim had just finished reading my paper about MacArthur.)

"Must be," I said. "She was back in two minutes."

"Did she lay it on you right then?"

"No. No. We needed more time for the torture. You know, of course, that under every black board there's a place for the chalk, a thin receptacle. Well, the Twinkie had the paddle in her hand. I actually believe she was frightened of it. She'd taken it from the display case in the hallway. It had been standing there next to two small plastic trophies our grade school had won sometime back in history.

"She placed the paddle vertically among the various pieces of chalk. My classmates were now gawking around each other's heads to see the paddle. I glanced over at Wilhelmina, seated there on my left. She was terrified. Didn't she know there hadn't been a spanking in this county for 60 years? Should I maybe go up and tell the Twinkie this? Should I perhaps give her a sweet hug and whisper that teachers do not whack their students here in America any longer?"

"No, no." Kim said, "Take your medicine and get on with it!"

"But it's not so easy. The Twinkie really was scared. She stared at the paddle for a few seconds, then stepped backward two full steps. I raised my hand. Ms. Roundtree finally noticed me."

"I asked, shouldn't we be using the big 'ram' word along with the paddling? She didn't answer. She just kept staring at the paddle like it's an overly plump rattlesnake."

"Listen," Kim said. "If you don't end this story pretty quick I'm going to whack you myself!"

"Okay, okay," I laughed. "Here's what finally happened that day. In order for me to be spanked we needed a paddle. I stood and marched up to the black board like a soldier, took the paddle and handed it to Ms. Roundtree. Then I bent over Wilhelmina's desk and gazed deeply into her eyes. I gave her a big wink as I awaited my punishment. Just as Ms. Roundtree barely touched my butt with the paddle, I yelled out, RAMIFICATION!"

"Our class erupted with clapping and sustained vocal applause. I took the paddle back from Ms. Roundtree and returned it to the trophy case in the hall. I came back to my desk and glanced at Wilhelmina. I saw she was already deeply in love with me."

"After school as I walked back toward my home, I heard Wilhelmina calling out to me. I turned around, waiting for her to catch up. I noticed she had a small dictionary taped to her left wrist."

"We need to talk," she said. "There's something bothering me."

"Okay, let's sit on your big front porch swing as usual." I glanced at the dictionary, wondering what it was for. I thought, this girl can't be so naive she's trying to stir me up about the 'F' word?

Kim was frowning at me. "This is not going to be a naughty story, is it?"

"Why should you care? You have one of the naughtiest mouths in all of Christendom. But no, it's not. It's an uplifting love story. My name is the same as the Archangel's remember? I'm in control!"

"However, no sooner were we sitting on Wilhelmina's front porch swing, than she changed her tune."

"You know, I really believe we should continue this conversation out in my big forest," she said.

"She had always called it 'her forest,' even though it was 10 miles long and five miles wide, and she didn't own a foot of it. I was already looking carefully at her muscles."

"What are you staring at?" Wilhelmina asked.

"Your muscles. They're impressive. I really think I should feel them."

"Go ahead. I don't care."

After feeling her muscles I had no worry. "What about the forest?" I asked. "Do you really want to see it?"

"Yes, of course."

Three hundred yards toward the forest she mentioned the dictionary. "Now we need to work our way up to the G's," she said.

"The G's" I echoed. "We'd better go back to your house and get a light. Thank heavens there's no school tomorrow because we're going to be in your forest for at least 30 hours! Sure we don't need a light?"

"No, no. Let's go on and do the best we can."

"But I was thinking, either Wilhelmina has had the 'word' but then lost track of it, or never had the right spelling in the first place. But I knew one thing, any boy in my class could find Wilhelmina's 'word' in about 15 seconds. We went into the forest about half a mile and sat down under the biggest tree we could find. Our shoulders were touching. You're lucky, I was thinking, sitting here in a deep, dark forest with the prettiest girl in your class. And with a dictionary, to boot."

"We'll trade it back and forth," Wilhelmina said, meaning the book.

I flipped around in the A pages. "Here's 'apple,'" I said. "Is that important?" But this is really not fair, I thought. I wonder what's bothering her about 'the word'? And should I even be discussing 'the word' with her? Could this be just a game? Maybe she's teasing me? She seems serious though. We were in the B's when I decided enough was enough. I took the dictionary and wouldn't give it back to her.

"What's wrong, we're only in the B's."

I gazed at her. "We don't need the dictionary any longer."

"Why not?"

"Because…I glanced at the sky through the trees, looking for strength. Because, I'm going to kiss you now. Stand up." I took her hand. We stood there three feet apart. I knew full well our lives were going to change and so did Wilhelmina. I stepped forward and took her shoulders. Strangely enough we didn't even bump noses. A full five-second kiss.

I looked at her later and saw she was in shock. Now what do we do? I wondered. Run for it, of course! "Wilhelmina, I'll race you back to your house, okay?" I was carrying the dictionary and I let her win by six paces.

"What do I do with the book?" she asked.

"Burn it!" I told her. "We don't need words any longer."

"Yeah! Yeah! Great!" Kim said. "You lost track of this Wilhelmina later, I assume. Hopefully."

"All a part of growing up," I told her, waving goodbye for this visitation. I met her father in the hallway and wished him well.

It was an early afternoon in late March. I grabbed the Glock 9 from my house, pocketed it in my jacket, and headed into 'the fields' again. I had absolutely no reason to go there today. I supposed I wanted to revisit the site of all the violence I had witnessed. At least that is what I told myself.

With the weapon in tow I don't have the slightest worry about walking through the tall grass. The first thing I wanted to see was if there was a police rope line around the spot where I found Kim that night. Coming within 80 yards of the place, I saw there was.

It appeared no one had bothered the setting, at least I saw no evidence of this. The color brown was still there, though. Kim's blood. It would have been nice to have been attacked at that moment, giving me an excuse to pull the Glock and put a couple of holes in the stranger with the paunch.

I walked around the police rope line three or four times and then covered most of the rest of the park, a stroll that took me approximately an hour. During this time I didn't meet a single person. Of course, school was still in session so no kids were around this early, but considering what had happened here recently, it's possible that young people were simply avoiding the park.

I returned to my house, dropped off the Glock, and headed for the hospital. Later in the evening I hoped to do additional research in the university library, looking for more information about Hawthorne. My paper was due in four days.

Approaching room 226 I happened to meet the physician and nurse just leaving. The doctor, who already knew me, suggested I might like to visit Kim for a while. He left the door open for me. I called to Kim, announcing myself, and also told her I planned to bring her 'play mother' in later for a visit.

"She won't come."

"This time she will. I promise." I sat down on a chair near her bed. "Now Kim, let's think back to your third meeting with Roberta. You've told me about your conversations while sitting on my front steps. I know about her riding in a police car. Now is there something else? Something you forgot about?"

"Sometimes a person doesn't know what to do."

"What in hell does that mean, Kim?"

"Remember the first day you visited me in this room, Michael? Do you remember what I told you?"

"Of course. You said, 'All is fair in love and war.'"

"But do you believe it yourself?"

I scarcely hesitated. "I guess I believe it for adults. I'm not sure about 13-year-olds."

She hesitated for a few seconds. "As you know, I didn't like Roberta. She wasn't right for you. But if I could, I would bring her back. I want you to know that."

"Now, what the devil are you suggesting, that you killed Roberta yourself? If so, who was the man with the paunch? Could this man have been Paul Stipanovitch by chance? And yes, I believe the attacker was a man. A person can't hide much hair under a stocking cap."

"The woman could have been a butch." Kim said, half in jest. "Okay then, a man. I'll at least pretend this is true." She paused again. "But no, it wasn't Paul."

"Then let's admit the truth here. The reason the killer wants you dead is because some way, somehow you have information that will put him away for life for the murder of Roberta Simms. We just don't have the smarts to figure out what this is. But I can tell you one thing, the man with the paunch was interrupted by someone that late afternoon. Otherwise he would have made certain you were dead before he left 'the fields'!"

"Now just relax here for a while." I touched her hand. "I'm going to drive to your home now and stuff your mother into my Ford, whether she likes it or not!" I raised my hand and waved goodbye.

Later I parked on the east side of Kim's home, exactly where Lorna and I had sat talking the night after the horrible attack when she was so distraught she could not drive. I walked around to the front of the house and knocked firmly on the door. No one answered. After 10 minutes I gave it up and walked completely around the house, checking every door and window available.

On the northeast side of the house was a double window looking into the garage.

Naturally I tried to see if Lorna Worthington could have taken her BMW and gone out shopping. I was almost hoping this was the case. But no, all three cars were snug in their places. Stan Worthington had already taken his Mercedes, which was the fourth car.

But then, God Almighty, the door from the house opened and Lorna staggered out toward her sedan. It's true the car was an automatic, but I was still not going to allow this drugged-up woman to drive away in her condition. She'd be in a wreck before she had gone five blocks. My car was well out of the way from her backing out of the garage, but I thought it was still better that I stood outside in order to flag her down.

I heard the BMW's motor running and waited for the garage door to open. It never happened. Half a minute passed. Thank God Kim had long since placed a garage door opener in my car's glove compartment. I reached in and took it out. I punched it hard. I punched it again. If this damned thing doesn't work, I'll have to race around to the north side and break my shoulder smashing through the small, weaker door there!

Finally the garage motor started and the door slid upward. Although she hadn't breathed enough carbon monoxide fumes to matter much, I climbed in from the right side and killed her motor immediately.

"What do you do?" Lorna began. "Keep waiting around here just to save people?"

For whatever reason, I can tell she's angry. I decided against a confrontation. She wasn't thinking clearly now. "Have you heard from the hospital today?"

She stared at me. "Oh your precious Kim. Always Kim. How did you happen to stumble into our lives? Do you even remember? Now give me back my car keys!"

Instead, I gave her a half smile. I held up the keys, practically in front of her nose. "They're going into my pocket," I told her. "All of your keys are going into my pocket."

She laughed. "You're really not a very nice person."

"Sometimes 'tough' is better than 'nice.'" The collapse will soon be coming, I thought. Play it straight and true. We don't need more complications.

"If I had a gun, I might blow you away."

"There's always Kim's Luger," I said. "I've heard she has little bullets and they really sting."

My left arm was resting across the seat, my hand just above her head. Do you have the will power for this game? I asked myself. It's totally silent here in this garage. Brace yourself, Mister. Let's see if you can live up to your name.

The car keys were still in my right hand. When she threw herself at me I dropped them on the floor boards. She doesn't seem much like Raggedy Ann now. Good God! She's struggling for all she's worth, trying to reach my mouth.

I held her so tight she couldn't really maneuver, and my mouth was higher than she could reach. "If you relax," I told her, "I'll pretend it's your birthday."

She tried to look up at me. I patted her arm a little. "All you need to do is relax, Lorna," I said.

She actually tried it.

"Now, after the birthday kiss, we'll need to stop and talk. You promise?" Her head scarcely moved.

It was a beautiful kiss, maybe because I was thinking of Kim at the time, and Kim certainly stopped me from focusing on sex. I suddenly realized that in all the months I had known Kim, I had never had one sexual thought about her. I almost laughed. That's not surprising because she's still such a tall, skinny shrimp!

I squeezed Lorna's arm again and told her we were going for a drive, and also mentioned we would be stopping for coffee.

"When do I get to drive?" she asked.

"As soon as you stop taking so damned many pills." I finally persuaded her to leave her BMW and walk outside to my own car. I closed the garage door behind us.

"Nothing will change," she told me.

"You never know. This was only a baby step. Nothing more." I gave her hand a pat.

"You didn't even acknowledge me," she said quietly.

I paused. "My God, Lorna, I'm 18 years old. You would have just been disappointed. I don't know the first thing about making love to a woman," I said, forgetting about Roberta Simms. I glanced out the window as we headed toward the hospital.

As we pulled into the parking lot Lorna immediately asked why she should be forced to visit here. "Trust me," I told her. "It's important."

She didn't argue much. I figured she had taken so many pills she would agree to almost anything. I hadn't realized that she was thinking clearly about some things, however. She already knew that before this day was over she would lure me into Kim's own bedroom and have her way with me there. Of course, I didn't know this until later.

"We need to go down this hallway," I told the woman who had just grabbed me in her BMW. We were, of course, on the second floor of the hospital by then.

"What's down this hall?"

"Don't be so dense, Lorna. Surely you know. How are you feeling now?"

"Not well. Actually, about the same." We kept walking.

We opened the door to Kim's room. No one was there to stop us. "Michael," Kim said. "You've brought mother."

"Yes, I promised I would." I led Lorna to the chair by Kim's bed. "Relax here for a while," I said.

Lorna took Kim's hand. "Are you feeling better, Kim?"

"Yes. But you know, my arms were broken. Of course, overall I'm better. They're letting me go home early next week."

"So soon?"

"Yes. Thank goodness."

"Michael kissed me in my BMW," Lorna said suddenly. By now she had removed her hand from Kim's.

Kim smirked at this news. "That's great, mother. It brings joy to my heart. Michael's a terrific kisser."

"I bet you don't believe me."

"Oh, but I do. You're so beautiful any man would like to kiss you. I've always admired you. I've told Michael this."

I glanced at Kim. "I'll be back later this evening," I said. "I'll bring my laptop and work on my large paper here in the hallway after I've seen you."

"Should you really be with Kim in the evening?" Lorna asked me.

"We'll be all right," I said.

"What's this all about, mother?" Kim asked.

"I've been thinking Michael shouldn't teach you any longer. When he picked me up I actually think he opened the garage door himself. He also swiped my keys."

"This will all work out," Kim said. "I'm certain Michael was just trying to help. It's what he does best." She looked up at Lorna and smiled. "Have you taken your correct number of pills today?"

"Of course. Why do you ask?"

"Well, you mentioned Michael might have opened the garage door himself. Perhaps he did this because you had turned on your car motor and were sitting alone in the closed garage. That's dangerous. Father told me he's been worried about you doing that before."

"There's too much thought of me," Lorna said. "I believe I can make it on my own."

"Perhaps a list might help," Kim said. "Like: turn on car, open garage door, back car out, close garage door. We could even have a poem as a reminder. Something like: if you follow the list, you cannot miss. Ha. Ha."

"I don't like that sort of thing, Kim. Good Lord, I should be able to back my car out of the garage without resorting to a poem."

"Well, maybe. But just remember to open the door before you back out. Otherwise, you will have a 'bunch of a crunch.' Ha. Ha." Kim paused and looked Lorna in the eye. "You and Michael will be leaving soon. Lean down here and give me a kiss."

"Yes, Lorna," I said. "That would be great. Kim won't bite you. I promise."

There was a long hesitation. Lorna looked at me, then at Kim. She finally leaned forward, little by little. Kim's mouth was basically free of bandages now and so that's where the kiss occurred. "I love you, mother. We must become even better friends. But don't be kissing Michael too much." She was grinning. "You should be kissing father. I think he's been missing you."

"I'll see you later, Kim. Come on, Lorna. Let's get you some coffee."

We were barely out of Kim's room, however, when Lorna whispered to me. "I don't want any coffee. I want you to take me home."

I considered this statement while we were walking. In the elevator I brought up the medications. "And you're certain you've taken all your pills today?"

"I've never taken any pill stronger than an aspirin in my life. Sure faked you out that morning in my kitchen, after Kim hit you in the head. Hell, I'll bet you thought I was a hippie."

Sure enough, I thought. But you're lying about the aspirin. Everyone knows you're some kind of addict.

As we approached my car I hit the power locks. She stopped and held onto my arm. "We do have an understanding, don't we?" she asked.

"Understanding?"

"I mean, you are coming in for a drink?"

"I don't drink much." I glanced at her hand still resting on my arm. She took it away. My face was still close to hers. "You may get me into bed, Lorna, but I'm not certain I'll ever fall in love with you."

"Maybe not, but I'll bet I addict you eventually! Hey, what about my door?" She was pointing.

I laughed. "Of course, your door. I'll be right there." I walked around and opened the door for her. Eventually I climbed into the driver's seat and we headed back to our own neighborhood.

"Don't you want to know why I'm doing this?"

"I already know why. You've decided you can't stand your husband in bed any longer, and you haven't had sex for more than two years. But might there not have been easier ways? Faking it in bed, for example? Or, what about divorce?"

"Still, the same old problem. Money. He's always controlled it. By the way, there are millions upon millions."

"Where did your husband find you?"

"New Orleans. Not always a good choice." She laughed. "I was hostess in a large waterfront restaurant. Twenty years old at the time." She glanced over at me. "What do you plan to do with me this afternoon?"

"Oh, probably play it by ear. Frankly, I really don't care what happens. You see, I've begun to like your husband, and to tell you the truth, I'm feeling sorry for him now."

As we drove up on the east side of her house, I was shaking my head in astonishment at the change in her demeanor. She seemed a totally different woman than the one who had accompanied me from the hospital just after Kim had been attacked.

"I know you feel I'm immoral, but I've been in this family for only three years. I'm not Kim's mother. Her real mother divorced Stan Worthington six years ago. Kim has actually tried hard with me. I mean, really hard. Half an hour ago you heard her ask me for a kiss. But her father's not the man you think he is. He's at best a benevolent dictator. I actually don't know what I'm going to do. Now, do you want to come in?"

I shrugged. "Sure, I'll join you. I must warn you, though, you've shocked me to such an extent, I may not be functioning too well at first. We may have to just talk for a while."

"Talk is fine. I need somebody to hold me close. But I'll bet you like me a little more now, since I've told you all these things."

"Maybe. Though, while I know why I want to be with you, I still don't understand why you're interested in someone 18 like my-self."

"You seem a strangely mature 18-year-old to me."

"Well, we'll see."

We walked into the house and I closed the garage door behind us. "This way into my bedroom," she said. After taking off our clothes, I told her she was beautiful.

"I know it," she said. "So what?"

As soon as her head was resting on my left arm, she asked if I had not been shocked when Stan Worthington hired me the night of Kim's birthday party and gave me an expense account. "Of course, I only learned of this the following day," she said. "Kim still knows nothing about it."

"Of course I was shocked. I guess I thought Kim was giving the two of you such a rough time you'd try anything to bring some peace and quiet into your lives."

"Yes, Stan wanted to make my life easier. As I told you, his other wife left him. He's already afraid I'll do the same thing. I can't stand him touching me. He's worthless in bed."

"Again, couldn't you have faked it a little with him and gone forward as best you could?"

"Not possible. Men don't understand such things. Here, let me hold you close against my breasts." She patted my shoulder. "You know, we're going to need more money. A lot more money. My husband will have to give you a substantial raise. And we can't allow Kim to get in our way, either."

"Okay, if you say so," I answered with little enthusiasm. "But to be honest about something else, everything 'mental' with you couldn't have been faked; the driving, the shaking of the hands, the pretending to be a hippie. I know you take a bunch of pills every day. I just don't know where the dividing line is."

"Why don't we just not worry about it for the moment?"

"All right. But it's possible that if you could get off the drugs a little, you might actually like your husband more."

"That seems silly to me."

"I'm not so sure. Better consider it. Here, give me your hand."

"So we hold hands? Perfect. Hey, might it help if I'd moan for you?" She laughed. "What does a guy like you need?"

I took a deep breath. "Oh, I'll probably just want to be close to you. Your soul mate." Now I was the one laughing.

She gently pushed me away from her. "Maybe we should see how we do."

"By all means. I'll bet you we do fine, just like the majority of people in the world." I kissed her hard on the mouth.

Lorna had told me the truth. I believe she planned to addict me. And by the time she was pretty much exhausted, I was already a little in love with her.

But then, on the left side of my pillow, I saw something astonishing. It shocked me so much that for several seconds I couldn't move. It was a typical long envelope, addressed to me from Roberta Simms. Across the face of this envelope, superimposed over my address, was a phrase that said: 'ALL IS FAIR IN LOVE AND WAR.' The envelope must have bounced out while Lorna and I were making love. It was still unopened and had been under Kim's pillow for God knows how long.

I touched Lorna's shoulder. "Lorna, this is Kim's bedroom. Look, an envelope addressed to me from Roberta Simms. Why did you bring me to this room? Jealousy? Of a 13-year-old girl? Getting back at her? God Almighty!"

"So I goofed up. Well, at least you finally received your letter. I guess you'll be going now." She'd been speaking as though half asleep.

As yet, I didn't completely understand the situation so I wasn't going to raise hell about it for the moment. "Please remember though, Lorna, Kim will be coming home next week. I would appreciate it if, before then, you could change the bedding here in this room."

Lorna turned to me then. "Why don't you change the bedding? After all, she's your little sweetheart."

I stopped at my house with the letter. I made certain I had all of my Hawthorne pages secure in my briefcase for my work later in the hospital, and then sat down on the sofa with the letter. Across the front of the envelope in Kim's firm hand was: 'ALL IS FAIR IN

LOVE AND WAR.' I caught the postmark. My Lord, Roberta must have been killed within two days of Kim receiving this missal. I tapped the envelope on a small end table nearby until I saw I had created a bit of space at one end. I took a pair of scissors and carefully trimmed the end away. I took a piece of Kleenex and used it to pull the letter free. I was praying to God this was just a cheerful note from Roberta, which meant nothing, but I doubted I'd be so lucky.

It was a full-page hand written letter and the slightest glance put me in shock. Had Kim given me this letter on the day it was handed to her, I could have saved Roberta's life. But how do I get this single sheet of paper to the police? I mean, where has it been all this time?

Was there still some snow in my back yard? If so, I might be able to slide this letter under some of it, get it moist, and then race it to the police. There's no way to put this off. They'll go and apprehend the killer tonight. But there's one thing I know, this information will never go on Kim's 13-year-old head. That would finally be too much! I simply won't do it!

Looking out the kitchen window I saw there were still patches of snow around. I opened the kitchen door and walked to the nearest patch. I slid the page under the snow, moistening it, and returned to my house by approximately the same path. Now I'm going to read the page carefully before turning it over to the police. I did this at my kitchen table.

I was thinking over the situation. I can't believe there's any advantage in waiting. The letter had been folded and was somewhat crumpled from Kim's head. It's certainly moist enough now. I need to drive down to the station. God, I hope Cramer or Wonderlich is on duty tonight.

I would have liked to have made a copy of the letter, but I dare not do it. If the police knew about the copy they'd be displeased, to say the least. No, the most intelligent move on my part is to turn the letter over to them, give them the 'lie' about how I found it, and then walk away. Should they want me to lead them to the place of the discovery in my yard, I'll be happy to take them there.

I found Wilson Cramer still in his office. Thank God! When he saw me he began laughing. "What's happened? Been arrested for smooching that skinny girl again?"

"Don't tease about that. Poor Kim is still in the hospital, at least until next week. No, I think I just broke your case wide open. Here, read this." I handed him the moist letter. "That's the signature of Roberta Simms. I'd know it anywhere."

*Dear Michael,*

*I'm in grave danger and believe I may soon be killed. Ten years ago my present stepfather married my mother and almost immediately began molesting me. I was eight years old at the time. Although I've begged him to stop, he's refused, and though I now have my own apartment, it makes no difference. He just comes here and takes me at will.*

*Today I'm coming to your house, begging for help. I want you to go with me to the police. Perhaps I made a mistake, but I've warned my stepfather that if he doesn't stop bothering me I'll turn him over to the authorities. As I'm sure you remember, I was never allowed to have my own car. It was one of the ways this BEAST controlled me. It's only because of a friendly cop that I'm able to get to your place at all. He doesn't know my situation, but he's still willing to drive me around. I think the officer likes me.*

*If I don't find you at home, perhaps I could tape this letter to your front door, or give it to your young friend, Kim. My biggest worry is that he's now following me, even when I'm in a police car. Once I saw him on the road right outside your house. I realize my situation is desperate, Michael, but I know you'll help me if you can.*

*Much love,*

*Roberta*

*P.S. My mother's a weak woman who can do nothing. She lives in fear!*

"My God, and we hadn't even suspected." He glanced up at me. "Where's the envelope?"

"There was no envelope. This letter was sticking out of the snow in my back yard. I pulled it from there less than half an hour ago. Do you want to drive over to my house and see where I found it?"

"Probably tomorrow morning."

"Look at these words. I bet Roberta Simms was killed almost immediately. I hope you'll share this information with Detective Wonderlich. Good God, had I received this letter I could have possibly saved Roberta's life."

"But no envelope was nearby?"

"Not that I could see this evening."

"I'll bet the stepfather has a paunch."

"Naturally."

"And he almost killed the young kid." Cramer paused. "Why was the stepfather worried about the girl?"

"She had no idea. I was standing there in her hospital room when Wonderlich questioned her. She had no idea how she came into 'the fields' that day."

"There's a great deal of linkage in this case. You, Roberta, her mother, the stepfather, Kim, her stepmother and her father, who hired you. But I want the envelope. There has to be one." Cramer glanced back at the letter. "There's something wrong here, my friend. Roberta's letter had been folded. It had been in an envelope. Again, I need that envelope."

I met his eyes. "Want to go and search for it? By now we'll need a powerful light."

"Tomorrow's better. Today I believe we should be visiting with Roberta's stepfather."

At that moment Wonderlich walked into the office. "Anything new?" he asked.

Cramer gave him the letter. "Michael appears to have broken the case."

"My God, the stepfather. Big businessman as I recall. Who would have thought?" He glanced over at me. "Is this her handwriting?"

"Yes. I'll swear to it. May not be necessary, though. The department already has samples of Roberta's handwriting. Her diary, remember?"

"Where was this letter found?"

"I saw it sticking out of the snow in my back yard from my kitchen window. I walked outside and grabbed it. I would bet you both that Roberta died the day after this letter was written."

Wonderlich was examining the paper carefully. "It was folded and in an envelope. Where is the envelope?"

"We wish we knew," Cramer said.

"How do you think this all came down?" Wonderlich asked me. "You've heard me ask such a question before."

"As the letter states, Roberta was being driven to my house by a policeman. She stated specifically that she'd also seen her stepfather near my house. Within two days the man somehow lured her 200 yards into 'the fields' and killed her."

"But why did he attempt to murder the child later? What was the connection there? Better consider your answer carefully, Michael."

I followed his suggestion and thought about everything for more than a minute. "Okay, here goes," I said finally. "While the stepfather was beating Roberta to death in 'the fields' she screamed out that she had given a young girl named Kim Worthington a letter implicating him. Roberta was, of course, begging for her life. Upon hearing this, the man knew he either needed that letter, or Kim Worthington dead. Of course, he killed Roberta anyway."

"Makes sense so far," Cramer said.

"Kim was always on that street. She had met Roberta a third time. Roberta had come to the neighborhood to find me. As the letter states, she wanted me to go with her to the police. Roberta and Kim sat on my front steps and talked about many things that day, none of which had anything to do with murder. However, before she left (again in a police car) Roberta handed Kim this letter, telling her it was of vital importance to get the letter to me. The letter never arrived, until today. Can't you convict this man without the envelope? By now you already know he killed Roberta and severely injured Kim."

It was totally silent in the office. Both detectives were staring at me. "If you have an envelope," Cramer said finally, "you'd better be coughing it up. And quickly."

"Is the envelope in your car?" Wonderlich asked softly.

"Yes, but now the three of us have to decide what the hell to do with it. I'll get it." I walked out to my car. I'd known it was possible I would have to give it up, but I was hoping not. Jesus! Two minutes later I was back. "You may wish you'd never seen it," I said, tossing the envelope on the desk.

Cramer picked it up. "What the hell is this?" he asked me. 'ALL IS FAIR IN LOVE AND WAR'? That's different handwriting. Who wrote this, the murderer? The man with the paunch?"

"Or young Kim," Wonderlich said. "This is more her flavor."

"Wait! Wait!" This was Cramer now. "Michael, you'd better give us the entire story here and now, slowly and carefully."

"Sure you wouldn't rather burn the envelope and just move on? Arrest your man and close your case? Are you really certain you want me to talk?"

"I think you'd better tell us what you know," Wonderlich said.

"All right, I'll give it to you. But remember, I warned you." I took a deep breath. "When Roberta handed Kim the letter addressed to me, Kim didn't follow her instructions. Instead, Kim wrote that phrase on the front of the envelope and left it unopened under her pillow in her bedroom. It's been there all these weeks. I found the letter a little over an hour ago."

"Yes, just as you were making love to the beautiful Lorna Worthington (whom I'm still convinced is mentally disturbed) at which time the fateful envelope bounced out from under a pillow." This has all been Wonderlich. Cramer was busy groaning with his head in his arms on the table.

Wonderlich continued. "Occasionally, intelligent young men come to the conclusion that it's sometimes necessary to limit the out-of-control lusts on the part of the females in their company. Birthday kisses in front of picture windows for all the world to see, and making love to other people's wives in their young girlfriend's bedroom. Michael, let me warn you, one day you're going to run out of luck! Now get the hell out of here and let us detectives work our case!"

"Okay. But I beg of you to consider the subject of the envelope carefully. Kim's been gravely ill, only 13 years old. You can convict the stepfather even if the envelope is burned. I urge you to do just that. Burn it!" I told them this on the way out to my car.

I remembered that I was being paid by Stan Worthington for a couple of hours of time in the hospital visiting Kim. Later in her room, I naturally said nothing about finding Roberta's letter, even though I knew she would eventually realize it was gone.

The doctors and nurses know me so well by now they don't even complain when I stay in Kim's room indefinitely. When Kim finally fell asleep I simply stayed there near her and returned to my work on Hawthorne's *The Scarlet Letter*.

Much later at home I checked the 10:00 news and soon saw video footage of Roberta's stepfather being arrested at his home and led out to a police car. And yes, the man did have a notable paunch.

I was dead tired. The pay was good, but I was getting at most five hours of sleep a night. Tomorrow (Saturday) was the same. I was scheduled to meet Kim both in the morning and in the afternoon. I hope I'm smart enough not to drive up that hill again to visit a certain gorgeous girl from New Orleans who had seduced me earlier. A young man has no chance with such a creature. God Almighty! I'm asleep within minutes while pondering this.

Entering the hospital just after 9:30 Saturday morning I was amazed to see Ben Zuckermann coming out of the cafeteria and into the lobby. As soon as he noticed me, he waved me over to a table he had already occupied. He was holding several sheets of paper in his left hand. I sat down next to him.

"So, you can relax now," he began. "Your case is closed. Well-known businessman diddling his own stepdaughter. Unbelievable. Wonder how the cops broke it?"

I shrugged. "When did you get back?"

"Three days ago." He paused. "My wife welcomed me home. Lost my secretary, though." He grinned.

"I tried to call you once. They said you were in Barbados."

"I'm meeting this morning with Stan. I hope you'll stick around. We're going to be discussing the kid. Kim, I mean. I've been up most of the night working on these papers." I noticed his left hand was stuffed full of them. "He's covering Kim with a trust fund, until she's 20. Thirty million dollars. You could be mentioned here as well. I mean, eventually. Stan should be coming along any minute."

I reminded Zuckermann about what he'd said once before about Lorna Worthington having a serious mental condition. He shrugged as though everything was still under consideration, including the mental stuff. At that moment Stan Worthington joined us. We shook hands and then returned to the cafeteria for coffee.

"Did you handle the situation with my wife?" he asked the

lawyer, after we were seated at a large table.

"Frankly, I have reservations about this plan. Are you really certain?"

"Jesus! Come on, Ben. She's had her chance!"

"I don't know. The plan could possibly backfire. There are too many uncertainties."

"We're discussing the situation with my wife," Stan told me. I nodded, but made no comment.

Ben Zuckermann turned to me then. There are two items on the agenda this morning. Kim's inheritance and the future of Mrs. Worthington's place in the family structure."

"I know Kim is quite fond of her stepmother," I suggested.

"I'm aware of that," Stan said, "and I haven't ordered Lorna out of the house as yet. I just want her cut off financially at the time of my death."

"I still have questions," Zuckermann said. "How do you know, if you cut off her money, Lorna will even stay there. Kim's only 13 years old. Without Lorna in the house, everything falls on Michael, a college student."

"We somehow need to bring Michael into this. Let's think about it."

"Look, people," I said. "I'm fond of Kim and I'm willing to help. But think carefully about this situation. Kim evidently is slated to receive $30,000,000 at the age of 20. But in the meantime, Lorna, Kim and I are sitting in that big house on the hill, with four expensive automobiles, but otherwise, stone cold broke. Kim might decide to propose marriage at age 17, but I'm still broke. Stan, it seems to me you'd better decide to just stay alive. What's all this talk about, any-way?"

"Should I die in the next couple of weeks, how much money do you think you might need to run that big house for, say, seven years?" He was looking directly at me now.

"The numbers are revolving in my head, even as we speak. But let's consider the overall situation. During my undergraduate years Kim will be in high school. While I'm earning a Ph.D. she'll be in college. An important point for me is this: what kind of control would I have over the situation? And again, what are we discussing here? Has some doctor persuaded you you're about to die, Stan?"

Zuckermann laughed. "After he dies, you could always seduce Lorna, Michael. Provide her with a small allowance. She already has her nearly-new BMW. What more does she need, for God's sake?"

"You make it sound easy. Kim has a rather huge crush on me right now. Think she would put up with me playing around with Stan's beautiful wife? The last time Kim caught me with another woman she hit me on the head with a baseball!"

"Can't you control these two women, Michael?" Stan asked, laughing a little.

"I don't know. As I recall, you couldn't. That's why you hired me, and gave me an expense account."

"But Lorna eventually couldn't stand me. Don't know why. Actually, I tried my best."

"You speak of Lorna as though she's already gone," I said. "Don't give up on her, Stan. Give her a hug once in a while and see how it goes. By the way, I've already considered the numbers while we've been talking here. We can discuss them later."

"Well, get them down on paper, Ben. But only begin writing checks to people at the moment of my death."

Stan glanced far away now toward the large window on his left. "I found the beautiful Lorna in New Orleans working as a hostess in a large restaurant on the water there. She appeared so pleasant and fun loving. Twenty years old. Kim liked her, too, the minute we walked in the house together. But then the change. Had she always been on the pills? I don't know. It was like Denver, Colorado drove her to a kind of mental illness. No sex. No affection." He shook his head.

"Did you ever consider turning her over your knee and beating the hell out of her?" This from Zuckermann, of course.

"No, I'm not much of a beater. Do you beat your wife?"

"Not my wife, but my secretary, more than once."

I laughed. "And is your secretary still around?"

He shrugged. "Can't win them all, I've always said."

I gestured toward Stan. "My advice is to work on your health. Stay on the bright side. Be nice to your wife. Look, I'm going up to the next floor and visit Kim." I glanced at Zuckermann. "Good luck with the will. Looks like my fate is in your hands." I laughed a little.

"Right. I'll be talking with you soon. We'll go over the numbers."

Fat chance, I thought, stepping into the elevator. It'll never happen.

Upstairs I quietly slipped into Kim's room, only to find her sleeping. I didn't stay. The kid needs her rest. I'll visit her again later this afternoon.

I told myself I'm going to my own house and finish my Hawthorne paper, but I lost focus somewhere along the way and drove right by my house and on up the hill. Naturally. There's a gorgeous young woman residing there. This time Lorna does answer the door, but I immediately noticed a change in her demeanor.

"Good morning, Michael. Have you been to the hospital yet this morning? Seen Kim?"

"Hello, Lorna. I met with your husband and lawyer Zuckermann. We talked about the future a little." There was a decided freeze apparent in that doorway.

"Did you and Stan discuss money with the lawyer?"

"Yes. Actually, Zuckermann met me in the hospital lobby earlier and suggested I stay with him for the meeting with Stan. The three of us finally met in the cafeteria. Say, are we just going to stand here at the front door? Or what?"

A false little smile was staring back at me. "I guess it depends on what you plan to do with me this morning. I'm sure not up for any more sex. You wore me out yesterday. Of course, if you have information about financial matters, please come in." She stood away from the door.

For God's sake I thought. This Lorna is stoned to the gills. So much for my 'nothing stronger than an aspirin' girl. Christ, a person can't trust anyone anymore. I sat on a sofa in the second living room. She had plopped herself down in a large chair clear across the room.

"So," she said, "enlighten me about the money. What was said over there in that hospital this morning?"

I stared at her, shaking my head. Yesterday, sweet as apple pie, today cold as snow. As Kim said, this woman is messed up in the head. But I smiled at her anyway. "So, you'd like information about the money situation."

"Well, I thought that's what we were here for."

I was getting a totally blank stare from across that room. So help me, if Lorna keeps giving me the cold shoulder, I believe I'll take Zuckermann's advice, turn her over my knee and lay a few on her! But for the moment I'll keep my word and talk about the money. I smiled over at her. She only stared back.

"Well, here goes. At age 20 Kim is slated to receive $30,000,000. They're talking about me being involved somehow, too, but I don't know. Upon Stan's death, if he ever dies!" I laughed, "the two of us are to run this big home together, take care of the four cars, and control general expenditures until Kim takes over. But I'll be honest with you. I think Stan is just blowing smoke. I doubt I'll ever receive a penny from this family, nor have any meaningful personal control."

"What else? Surely I was discussed individually, too."

I smiled at her again, which probably made things worse.

"You are to receive nothing, Lorna. Now Zuckermann was arguing about this, stating such a ruling would never hold up in court, but so far Stan is sticking by his guns. See what happens to women who play the 'cold fish role' for nearly three years?"

"Please leave this house immediately!"

I walked over to where she was sitting and looked down at her for several seconds.

"Going to beat me now? You know, rather than take a beating from you, Mr. 18-year-old, I would rather just strip naked and go lie on Kim's bed and let you take what you want. I warn you, though, you'll get no encouragement or affection from me!" She stood up, glaring at me.

I grabbed her and kissed her hard on the mouth, causing her to collapse backward again. She came right back up against me though, smiling. "It has to be Kim's bed," she said. "I insist. I told you I would eventually addict you." In spite of what she had said earlier, she continued stroking my right arm all the way into the bed-room.

Although she was stoned to high heaven, she finally did what she could. After climaxing a couple of times, she began crying what for me seemed almost forever. It shook me up drastically. I told her I loved her over and over, for almost an hour. Kim would hate us for what we were doing here!

In spite of the strong feelings I have for Lorna, I do not have much faith in this relationship over the long run. In all honesty, I would be just as happy if she returned to her husband, gave him some honest affection and made him a contented man. I wish I could persuade her to give this a try. Kim will be home from the hospital in two days and God knows what's going to happen then.

I suddenly began laughing. "Lorna, you told me yesterday I was supposed to ask your husband for a substantial raise. You told me we needed a lot of money, and that we couldn't allow Kim to horn in on our time. Strange how everything eventually plays out. What are your real plans, sweetheart? I think we should discuss them." I glanced around the room. Good lord, we were still in Kim's bed, which scared the hell out of me. In spite of this, I continued holding Lorna close to me, which I hoped gave her some comfort.

"Do you think Stan might eventually give me some money?" she asked finally.

"It could happen, especially if he's pressured by Zuckermann, but in the meantime I wish you would try and make your husband happy. It wouldn't kill you. In this day and age, women should be playing every angle."

"I tried to explain this to you yesterday, why it was difficult."

"To hell with that attitude! Good God, Stan wouldn't put much pressure on you. Not like I did. We've been together a couple of days and I immediately saw I was, well, too energetic. When you seduced me, I'll bet you were hoping I'd collapse after three or four minutes and leave you in peace." I laughed again. "It was never going to happen. And if we had stayed together, I would have been grabbing you practically every damned day. You might have eventually become annoyed with me."

"I don't know. Perhaps I should take off. Go back to New Orleans."

"Oh, for God's sake, don't do that. You know, Kim told me something once. She said, 'only our pretending is important.' This is your charge, Lorna. I want you to pretend. Start hugging and kissing your husband a little. He's a decent man. If you can't concentrate on the sex, just remember to keep rubbing his shoulders nicely all the while. Maybe even moan a little. It should work out."

"Are we still going to be friends?"

"Lorna, you surely know how much I care for you. How much I've enjoyed being with you. Of course, we're going to be friends. And I imagine I'll be able to help you with the money, too. Zuckermann is siding with me. I'm not going to allow Stan to close you out. But you simply have to give him a little affection. These are games people sometimes have to play."

"But we won't be able to be together anymore."

"Let's play it by ear. Who knows what will happen? But concentrate on your husband for a while. That would make me happy."

"Why, for heaven's sake?"

"Because I don't like you constantly breaking his heart. Trust me, I know what I'm doing." I held her close to me now and kissed her gently for a long time. "I want you to do me a favor," I said finally. "I want you to start cutting back on the pills a little. Please. This might help your life in other ways."

"Okay, I'll do my best." She eventually walked with me to the door holding fast to my hand. "Do you think we can stay strong?" she asked. "Stay moral?" She smiled up at me. "I hope to hell we never stay strong. And now you know my feelings!"

"I like it that you care for me," I told her, trying not to be too specific.

Driving away from the large home I was in a good mood and was ready to stop at my own house and begin work on the ending of my large paper. My hope is to turn it in sometime on Monday. I made a ham and cheese sandwich, poured myself a large glass of milk, and continued working on and off for three hours.

By the end of this time my positive attitude had changed somewhat. Although I was pleased with my work on the paper, my feelings about the Worthington family had begun to unravel. By now I felt trapped. Kim will be home from the hospital in two days and may well discover that a letter is missing from under her pillow, and also that someone has been bouncing around on her own bed.

Stan Worthington was constantly pressuring me to look after Kim, even as I allowed myself to be seduced by his young wife yesterday. Nor is this relationship really over yet. I gave Lorna some good advice today, but her last words let me know she was basically ignoring me. As regards 'morality' she said: "I hope to hell we never stay strong." I wonder when I'll be forced to begin lying to this family. And now, well, it's about time to look the young dragon in the eye. The hospital beckons.

Ten minutes later when I approached room 226 I heard the television was on. As soon as Kim saw me walk in she turned off the TV and told me in a firm voice that the stepfather of Roberta Simms had been arrested for her murder.

I nodded as I sat down by her bed. "I've already heard about it. I'm assuming he's the same man who attacked you."

"Yes, complete with the paunch."

I leaned down and kissed her. "I never met Roberta's stepfather, though sometimes such men are notorious for molesting their young stepdaughters."

"How do you think the police caught him?"

"One never knows. Her own mother might have turned him in. Perhaps she knew what he had done to her daughter, and her conscience was bothering her."

"I'm glad it's over."

"So am I." I grinned at her. "Ready to go home Monday?"

"I'm ready right now. Have to get back and keep 'play mother' from grabbing you." She laughed. "Lorna's in love with you, Michael. You surely know this. The question is what are we going to do about it? She's so damned good looking she can roll over any young man she meets, including you!"

"You don't believe I can stay strong?"

"Hell no! She'd grab you in three minutes flat with her soft little drug-infested voice. What we need to do is cut her back on the pills and then ease her into my father's bed. If she doesn't like the sex, let her fake it. But she had better get with it and become a normal wife, or father is soon going to bounce her butt right out of that house. Can't you do something, Michael? You're the strong silent type."

"I could try, but according to you, getting too close to Lorna might be dangerous."

"What was that business about the 'kiss' she mentioned here in my room? Did she just grab you, or what?"

"Are you certain you're really interested in this?"

"Of course. I guess it had something to do with the garage door. Her BMW?"

"Well, I had knocked at the front door for several minutes Friday afternoon. You'll remember I was going to pick up your mother and bring her in to the hospital for a visit. I finally went around the house on the north side and looked into some of the windows that opened onto the garage. Almost immediately Lorna staggered out of the house into the garage, climbed into her BMW, and turned on the motor."

"But the garage door never opened."

"Exactly. At first I waited, but after a couple of minutes I grabbed the opener you had put in the glove compartment of the Ford and hit it twice. Finally the door opened. I raced inside, jumped into the BMW on the right side and killed the engine. Lorna was not pleased with me. 'What do you do?' She asked. 'Keep waiting around the house just to save people?' By now I had her BMW keys in my right hand. She told me that, having stolen her car keys, 'I wasn't such a nice guy after all.' I said, 'sometimes tough, was better than nice.'"

"Good Lord, she must have been completely zapped on drugs. How did you deal with the situation?"

"I remembered back to the day of your 13th birthday, the day I kissed you in front of my window. I told Lorna that I would pretend it was her birthday and kiss her, but then she would have to immediately calm down. It was a nice kiss, probably because I was thinking about you at the time." I smiled at her. "But that's about the whole story. Lorna got out of the BMW and into my Ford. I closed the garage door behind us and we came to meet you in the hospital. Once there, of course, she announced that I had kissed her in the car."

"This entire situation spells trouble. I'm worried that Lorna might never have opened the garage door at all. It's possible she might have kept sitting there with the motor running until she died. That's what my father has been worried about. Actually, you probably saved Lorna's life, Michael."

"Possibly. But her psychological makeup was strange, to say the least. At first I assumed she was suicidal. But when I noticed how angry she got, I was unable to keep up with her train of thought."

"When she was here, sitting by my bed, I sort of made fun of the kiss and the garage door fiasco, but I now realize the situation was dead serious. This woman is a danger to herself. Keep giving some thought to this, Michael. We have to help Lorna if we can."

"Lorna is one mixed up lady, Kim. I just don't know. But I have still another question for you. It's about your father's health. Do you know anything about some sort of problem he might have?"

Kim laughed. "He's a nervous Nellie. Don't pay any attention to him. He always thinks he's about to die."

"Okay, glad to hear it, I guess. For God's sake, Kim, give me another hug. We have to keep our own sanity in decent shape." She not only gave me another hug, but two sweet kisses as well.

After a good night's sleep I had a small breakfast and then drove to the hospital where I found Kim still fast asleep in room 226. I backed out into the hall again where I met Stan Worthington coming toward me after leaving the elevator. When I told him Kim was still asleep he suggested we pull up a couple of chairs and chat for a while. Not knowing what was coming, I slowly turned a chair around and faced him, looking directly into his eyes.

"You won't believe what I'm about to tell you regarding early this morning," he said by way of introduction. (Bet I will, I immediately thought). "It happened just after 2:30 in the early morning," Stan continued. "Lorna came into my room. I was half asleep, naturally, and frankly in shock. She remained with me for the rest of the night; in fact, she's still asleep in my bed as we speak. I can't tell you how pleased I am about this. It makes me wonder if I shouldn't be talking with Zuckermann again about her inheritance."

"That might be a good idea. Of course, I've never really understood what the situation is concerning Lorna, though Kim mentioned her drug problem, just as you did." (My God, I thought, it seems as though Lorna was following my orders precisely in this early morning hour.)

"Stan," I continued, "is it possible Lorna had begun withdrawing from the pills on her own, without us knowing about it? If so, it might explain why she paid you an early morning visit. Those many pills she was taking earlier were probably keeping her in a kind of stupor."

"It's possible, I suppose. Though I really don't know."

I gazed at him seriously. This conversation was actually making me uncomfortable. And, of course, I felt guilty. Stan Worthington is not only Kim's father, but also one of my best friends. I can't believe how muddled my own life has become. The pressure was wearing on me. For several seconds it was quiet in that hallway.

"You still seem concerned," Stan said. "Anything wrong?"

"No, nothing. Your report about Lorna's visit was uplifting; in fact, I think it might well usher in a new relationship between you and your young wife. Nothing could be more important. It will be great for Kim as well. Do you have any idea what might have led to this change in attitude?"

"No, I'm just glad it happened. It's certainly turned me into a happy camper."

I paused. "Now, as for me being concerned, well, there's other news and it's been on my mind for a couple of days. Have you heard the police finally solved the case of Roberta's murder? It was on television Friday evening. The killer was her own stepfather. I should have told you about this Saturday morning in the hospital cafeteria but, of course, we had other things on our minds at the time. I can still remember how concerned we all were after Roberta's murder. The stepfather was naturally the same man who attacked Kim, the one with the paunch. Anyway, this has been on my mind since Friday."

"Does Kim know?"

"Of course. I joined her in her room last evening just as she was watching the unfolding of the entire case on television."

"What about Lorna?"

"I'm not sure. I haven't discussed it with her. I must say, though, this is one of those rare times in one's life when everything appears to be moving in the right direction. Now, Stan, I have a large paper due tomorrow. I'm going to skip visiting Kim this morning, but I'll be back this afternoon. And you'll probably remember that I'm driving Kim home from the hospital tomorrow as well."

He reached for my hand. "How are things going in the university, Michael?"

"Oh, it's a struggle, but I'm doing okay. It helps that Kim is almost well now, and the news about Lorna seems nothing short of astonishing."

"I always rely on you, Michael," he said, grasping my hand more firmly now. I nodded to him and walked away at a measured pace.

I know how you rely on me, I thought, smiling a little as I stepped into the elevator. They all think because I know the entire history of the western world, and am now riding on a full scholarship at the university, that I'm also some kind of psychologist, always ready to solve any problems that come along in their lives, including sexual ones. Hell, considering the bedlam in my own life at present, someone should be sewing a 'scarlet letter' on my own chest right now. Maybe Kim will do that for me, just after she shoots me a few times with her little play Luger with the bullets that really sting.

Just before 5:00 on Sunday evening, when I was visiting Kim again, she had a suggestion I simply ignored, after having a good laugh.

"Kick off your shoes," she told me, "then jump into bed with your clothes on."

I sat down by her, took her hand and gave her a friendly squeeze. "No, I don't think so, Kimo. Not tonight, though it sounds like fun."

"But we never make any progress. How in hell can we possibly deal with our situation over the long run?"

"You explained it on the first day we met. Remember? We had walked up to your house and you showed me a picture of Lorna." I grinned at her. "You hadn't quite leveled with me, though. You said Lorna was who you would look like when you were 17, presenting her as your real mother. We decided there were about five or six years difference in our ages. You asked me what would happen to those years, and I said…"

"You said, probably gone in a flash."

"You remembered. I thought you might. But you see, this is our dilemma—those five or six years. It's why I can't join you in bed and do lots of other things as well."

"Like being trapped in the elevator at school when I wanted a kiss!"

"Exactly. But how do you think humanity will view our relationship when I'm 24 and you're 18?"

"No one will care what we do, or where we go, or even if we decide to get married. But let's be honest, we're discussing the same six-year spread here. My worry is that you may just get tired of waiting for me to grow up, and take off like Eugene Onegin in Russia."

I gave her a broad smile. "Or it could be that I like my own young Tatianna a lot more and won't go anyplace. But you know, Kim, the person who may eventually become bored with our present relationship could well be yourself. As I mentioned once before, an 18-year-old boyfriend can be a real drag for a 13-year-old girl."

"Remember what I told you the last time we were out for a cheeseburger? We go forward day by day. There's simply no other way to play it."

"Okay by me. As long as you're happy. By the way, while you were snoozing this morning I had a brief talk with your father out in the hall. Now we share just about everything, right?"

"I sure hope so."

"Anyway, very early this morning he had a special visitor."

"Lorna?"

"Yes. She was in an affectionate mood. I think we should both be pleased."

"To what do you attribute her change in attitude?"

"No idea. The important thing is, it made your father happy. He's even thinking about talking with Zuckermann again concerning Lorna's inheritance."

"Do you feel he can count on her to remain steady?"

"Let's cross our fingers and hope."

"I don't think you completely trust her."

"Maybe not, but what other choice do we have? I've already talked with her about cutting back on the pills. Of course, who knows if she's following my advice?"

"On the surface this seems too good to be true, but if my father told you, I guess we have to believe his story."

"I believed it. He was so happy it couldn't have been otherwise."

"Come down here," Kim said. "I need my good night kiss. A long kiss this time! Good," she said afterward. "But it would have been even sweeter if you would have kicked off your shoes and jumped into bed."

I grinned at her, but I waved this idea away. I told her I would see her tomorrow afternoon.

Later at home, I looked over my Hawthorne paper for the last time, caught the 10:00 news, and fell asleep in my bed. There is no rush tomorrow. I can sleep in.

My large paper was submitted to my advisor about 1:30 p.m., just before I dropped by to pick up Kim. Because of hospital rules, Kim was in a wheelchair, though she can actually walk fine. Kim's right arm was in good shape now, though her left arm was still in a sling and I always had to watch out for it. I have a suitcase and some additional clothing draped over my arm to take to the car.

We went down to the lobby in the elevator and left the wheelchair outside the front door as we had been instructed. Standing by the car I hugged Kim before she got in, and we took our time driving back to our neighborhood.

I was concerned about Kim, who appeared worried about something. Her hands were trembling and she was definitely pale. Since I know she has only positive feelings about her father, I can only think the problem relates to Lorna or myself. I had never seen Kim like this. I glanced at her again. My God, she appeared somewhat deranged!

Because of the double life I had been leading recently, I noticed I've become somewhat fatalistic, always fearing the worst. I once imagined Lorna and I had somehow lurched near a cliff in her BMW and were creeping ever closer to the edge. When I glanced back I saw Kim, with just her good right hand, easily shoving us over the top. Kim was laughing hysterically.

Twenty minutes later we pulled up on the east side of her home. I hit the left garage door opener and Kim went on ahead into the house. I took my time. I lifted the suitcase from the trunk and took some clothes out of the back seat, which had been on hangers. I walked through the garage and on into the house, finally coming into the second living room where I heard Kim talking to Lorna, who was flopped on a sofa.

"The dreamy beautiful girl from New Orleans, who broke my father's heart a thousand times. My own 'play mother.'" My God, Kim had taken a 22 semi-automatic pistol from a shoebox under her bed (a weapon I hadn't known existed) and was waving it around in the room. She already knew the truth. "You and Michael were in my bed."

"So? What's the problem? You weren't using it?"

"If you weren't such a total drugged-up loser lying there, I swear I would put one in your chest right now! And if you're smart you'll never mention the sex to anyone. My father is ready to throw you out of the house as it is!" She turned to me. I had already set the suitcase down on the floor and placed the rest of Kim's clothing on another sofa. "Follow along, Michael. We're going to Kimmie's room. To the pillow that hid the envelope from the world." She laughed a little. "Roberta was never good for you, Michael. I've told you that before."

"You still have your gun in your right hand, Kim."

"Just forgetfulness. Not to worry."

I followed her into her bedroom, where Lorna had been sobbing earlier in my arms.

"We are here, Michael. Finally free! But you should never have allowed 'play mother' to bring you here. Didn't you feel any danger at all?" She frowned. "I had always done my best for that woman. But she's a druggie all the way!"

"You still have your 22 hanging loose, Kim. Shouldn't you put it away?"

She only stared at me.

"It's strange," I continued. "I've never thought of you in terms of 'bed.' I've always loved you in another way." I knew it was a mistake when I saw the semi-automatic rise and was now leveled at my stomach.

"It's really too bad, Michael. You know? Cause you were always such a damned good kisser!"

I felt the first bullet. After that, I didn't remember much....

Kim gave me two shots in the stomach and one in the left leg. I suppose I may always be a bit crippled in my life because of that third bullet. Within seconds after drilling me, Kim ordered Lorna to call for an ambulance to save me. By the time they arrived, Kim was racing around the house screaming, from one staircase to another, like a crazy girl in a gothic novel. I learned of this later.

She fought the police to the last; it finally took three officers to bring her down. While there may have been differences of opinion regarding what transpired in that house, when the authorities arrived, many would conclude that Kim was, at least for the moment, mentally disturbed.

I, of course, was out of the picture, and for the first couple of days was bothered by no one except a doctor or two who were trying to get Kim's bullets out of my tummy or my leg. I later learned that Stan Worthington had early on ordered Ben Zuckermann on the scene, who had shut Kim's mouth down, giving her at least a chance of eventually pleading insanity for blasting me.

Drifting in and out of consciousness I was well aware that I have had extremely bad luck with women of late, with one dead, one crazy and the younger kid in jail, principally because of shooting me, the guy she supposedly loved. I recalled what I had thought weeks ago, the day Kim found Roberta's body in the fields, that Kim was the most violent individual I had ever known. At the time I was scared to death, suspecting she had actually killed Roberta herself.

Within four days I was out of my room and wandering all over the hospital, though still in a wheelchair. The wheelchair was principally because of that bullet in the left leg, which although extracted, could be a problem for some time to come. It was on the fifth day that I went to the cafeteria. I grabbed a Coke and was sitting over next to a window when I felt someone touch my right shoulder. It was Kim, backed up by Zuckermann. Kim no longer had a sling on her left arm. I smiled at her. "They've fixed up your arms. I guess I should have suspected that."

"They still have things they need to do with the left one." She was whispering now. "I'm so sorry, Michael!"

"I know. Have you finally understood why l hesitated there in your bedroom?"

"I think so. I must have been insane when I shot you."

"Probably." I turned toward Zuckermann. "When can we count on the trial beginning?"

"In a few days. There's not much sense in putting it off."

I glanced at Kim again, still whispering. "We've both been through a lot, Kid. You, beaten almost to death in 'the fields'; me shot three times by a young girl I've always loved in a special way." I laughed a little. "Did you ever make your peace with Lorna?"

Zuckermann had strolled away and was no longer listening to our conversation.

"That may be a problem. Remember in the hospital I told you she was after you. I imagine you believe me now. As you know, I almost shot her that Monday."

"I'm glad you didn't. Things will eventually work out, I suppose."

"Michael, I want to thank you for not pressing charges."

"Of course. What good would pressing charges have done?"

"To get revenge for your poor leg."

"Don't be silly." I called to Zuckermann again. "I imagine I'll be going on the stand."

"Almost certainly. I'm guessing you'll be the prosecution's main target. Seems unbelievable, since you were the young man who was shot, but that's the way it goes sometimes." He looked toward Kim. "I think we should be leaving soon. Why don't you meet me back at the car?" Kim nodded.

By the time Zuckermann was out of range, Kim was already crying. I took her right hand and gave it a squeeze. "Relax, Kimo. We'll get through this. But why do you think Lorna led me directly to your own bedroom? You surely know I didn't have the slightest idea where I was at first."

"Lorna wanted you, Michael. Also, she was jealous of me because of the inheritance situation. As I said, it may be a while before I can forgive her." Kim paused. "I feel so miserable now!"

"Lean down here, Kim. I'll give you a kiss that will live in infamy." Afterward she was laughing a little. "You stole Roosevelt's line from just after Pearl Harbor. Michael, even after being shot three times, you really are a damned good kisser!"

I gave her right hand a final squeeze and watched her walk away erect now, trusting I suppose that her history teacher still loved her at least a little bit.

We were meeting together in the Worthington home preparing for Kim's trial, which was slated to begin early next week. The principals were all in place—Kim, Lorna, Zuckermann, Stan and me. I'm out of my wheelchair now, though still limping a little. As for Kim, we hadn't seen each other since meeting that day in the hospital, the day she apologized for shooting me. Zuckermann was, of course, in charge of the meeting and began the discussion.

"Fred McKinsey is the lawyer who is going against us on Monday. He's an assistant district attorney, naturally on the side of the prosecution. I expect McKinsey might begin with a mild shot across the bow, namely the evidence of Officer Genavissie. He could go through that early morning meeting with Michael at his home, ending with the statement by Michael that Kim is a 'spitfire,' who likes all the kisses she can get, prefaced by the jarring words, 'Kim may tell you to go blank yourself!'" Zuckermann smiled. "This might have shown great solidarity between Kim and Michael, except since then Kim has shot Michael three times in her own bedroom. Naturally, McKinsey might not even call Genavissie. We just don't know."

Kim raised her hand. "This one statement about the 'kisses' leads one to believe that was all Michael and I ever did. It simply wasn't true."

Zuckermann opened his hands somewhat in exasperation. "Unfortunately Michael said those words that morning. I'll have to come back on cross examination to bring the situation back into a more believable stance." Zuckermann gazed over at me. "But the 'kisses' business was just the ending of the conversation that morning. Before that came the eight books on the kitchen table by Nathanial Hawthorne dealing with *The Scarlet Letter*, and Genavissie's strong hints that Michael and Kim are boyfriend and girlfriend. By now half the people in Denver will know that Michael is refusing to press charges against Kim, which means they're on the same side. Everyone will assume these two young people are in love."

Stan Worthington was now raising his hand. "How much should we go into the fact that I've hired Michael to teach Kim an hour each day, and that he has an expense account?"

"I'm still considering this. Right now, though, I need to know where the 22 semi-automatic and the ammunition were located in the home when Kim walked in."

"That's easy," Kim said. "Everything was in a shoebox under my bed, up toward the front. No one else knew about the gun."

"Any problem getting at it?" Zuckermann asked.

"None."

"And where exactly was Michael at this time?"

"Coming in from the car," Kim said. "Lorna was lounging on a sofa."

"When did you retrieve your twenty-two?"

"I don't remember," Kim answered. "I was distraught. Will I be taking the stand at my trial?"

Zuckermann considered. "How are your nerves these days?"

"Shot to hell!"

"Then I'm not putting you on the stand. McKinsey would have a picnic with you. And because he won't be able to get at you, Kim, Michael will be his principal target." He turned to me. "Anything in your recent past you might wish to amend?"

"Not really. As long as Kim stays off the stand, I think I'll be okay. What about the other case?"

"You mean Roberta's murder? Only the fact that Kim was horribly attacked later as well. The attack on Kim could have negatively affected her mental health. I must remember that aspect."

Zuckermann glanced at me again. "Help me out here, Michael, what will we be facing with most of the detectives on the scene?"

"Genavissie is the only one I know about who will be totally negative. Wonderlich knows that Kim has a violent side and is emotional. He might testify about the 'bloody nose' incident, or the 'baseball happening.'" I grinned at Kim. "Wilson Cramer I know fairly well. He's a straight shooter, a good officer, and I don't expect any problems there."

"What happened to my letter?" Kim asked suddenly. "The

one under my pillow?"

I looked at her, this time without smiling. "It was my letter, Kim. It was addressed to me."

"But Roberta gave it to me. And I want the envelope."

"Just forget it, Kim."

"So help me, Michael, sometimes I don't know about you!" She stomped her right foot a little.

"That's okay, Kim. Throw all the fits you like. I don't care."

Zuckermann was ignoring our little skirmish. He watched Kim as she stood and crossed quickly to the sofa where I was sitting and leaned against me. I did not take her hand. The lawyer stood and soon wished us all goodnight. Kim's father and Lorna left us as well, probably heading toward separate bedrooms, but who knows? Relationships change these days like gathering storms and blossoming rainbows. Kim and I sat there alone in partial darkness, hanging onto each other, wondering if we were ever going to be able to free ourselves from this damned mess.

The trial on Monday began in turmoil, with McKinsey arguing about the seating arrangement. I had been sitting beside Kim who was sitting next to Zuckermann. Stan Worthington had been on my right. Lorna was not with us, but was sitting far in the back of the courtroom.

McKinsey, in a loud voice, demanded I be disallowed from sitting next to Kim. When asked why by the judge, he reminded everyone that I was the man Kim had shot, and that he was presently trying her for this crime. The judge appeared to think this over and finally had me move one row behind Kim.

Actually, I thought McKinsey was correct in raising this point. Had I been allowed to sit by Kim throughout the trial, I would have never believed they were at all serious about the proceeding.

I had learned earlier that Judge Simon was partially deaf. He often had his left hand cupped behind his left ear. A minor point, perhaps.

The court stenographer, a rather plump middle-aged woman, was already in place ready to go.

At any rate, I didn't get to enjoy my new position behind Kim long, because I was called to the stand by McKinsey. He swore me in and began working me over.

"You are Michael Sheppard, university student. On Monday afternoon I believe you gave Ms. Worthington a ride from the hospital to her home near the university. What type of vehicle were the two of you in at the time?"

"A mid-sized Ford."

"Did you and Ms. Worthington enter the home together?"

"No. The home has a four-car garage. I had hit the power button for the extreme left door. As soon as it opened Kim entered the home alone. She met Lorna Worthington in the second living room."

"In your opinion, what was the relationship between Kim and Lorna Worthington?"

"I believe they cared for each other. On Friday afternoon in the hospital, when Lorna Worthington was sitting by Kim's bed, Kim asked Lorna for a kiss. Lorna leaned down and kissed her. This was the last time the two were together before Kim walked into her home on that Monday afternoon."

McKinsey paused for several seconds, as though considering something else. Mr. Sheppard, you do understand, do you not, that your relationship with Kim Worthington, a 13-year-old girl, is illegal?"

"Objection," Zuckermann said, before I could answer. "This is a trial dealing with bullets, not kisses!"

"Ha, kisses," McKinsey interjected softly.

"What was that, Sir?" Judge Simon asked, not quite understanding what had been said.

"Nothing, Your Honor. Nothing."

"And that last objection is sustained. Next question please."

"Mr. Sheppard, did you not have a previous girlfriend earlier this year who was brutally..."

"Objection, Your Honor. That case will soon be tried in another venue with another defendant, namely the stepfather of Roberta Simms."

"Sustained, for now, though we could revisit this subject later. I am presently studying the facts of this earlier case, especially regarding what happened to Kim Worthington later."

By now I realized that something was wrong with Lawyer McKinsey. I believed, not unlike Lorna Worthington on occasion, that this middle-aged man was stoned to the gills! Has no one else in the courtroom noticed this?"

"My next question, Mr. Sheppard, involves a fateful night a few weeks ago when you, in the dark of night, took a large flashlight and entered what is now known as 'the fields.' Can you explain to the court why you did this?"

"That's difficult to answer. Ms. Kim Worthington and I had a history lesson scheduled for that evening after school."

"Excuse me, Sir, would that have been in your small home down the hill?"

"No, in Kim's large home at the top of the hill."

"Naturally, because previously you had been observed kissing Ms. Worthington through a window in your own home. On that occasion the police actually dropped by to give you both a stern warning about such things going on."

McKinsey had paused again. It was obvious he was not in good shape.

"Now, Mr. Sheppard, please give a further explanation as to

why you went into 'the fields' in the dark of night."

"I became increasingly concerned as the evening wore on. Kim had not yet returned home."

"But, Mr. Sheppard, she is 13 years old. Surely if she can sustain getting kissed half to death, and her neck completely re-arranged because of the constant smooching, she should be able to stumble her way back home eventually."

"Objection, Your Honor. Can't we do something about this corrosive attitude?"

"Yes, we can. I want an immediate side bar."

Everyone left me in place with my perfect hearing. Because of Judge Simon's lack of hearing, the two lawyers were going at it full bore. I actually believe some in the first row of the courtroom could also hear what was going on. Judge Simon was leaning forward, with his left hand cupped behind his left ear. He is, of course, addressing Fred McKinsey.

"Now, Fred, it appears something is very wrong here. Do you need a 10 minute recess?"

"No, I believe we should go forward."

"Well, maybe. But I'm going to ask that you take a time out now and allow Mr. Zuckermann to cross examine for a while."

"My main problem is that I'm not allowed to question the girl."

"Well, we can't help that, now can we? Now if you have objections to any of Mr. Zuckermann's questions please feel free to express them."

"I hate this business!" McKinsey said softly.

"What was that?" the judge asked.

"Nothing. Nothing." McKinsey was already walking away, but he wasn't too far away from my acute hearing. "That damned little gun slinger over there drives me crazy!" he said half under his breath.

"Please ignore any interruptions, Mr. Zuckermann, and continue."

"Yes, Your Honor. Thank you."

"Mr. Sheppard, what did you eventually find in 'the fields' that evening?"

"Ms. Kim Worthington, horribly injured. At first I thought she was dead."

"What happened then?"

"I picked her up and carried her 200 yards to the street. Her father happened to meet us there driving by. We went immediately to the hospital."

"Side Bar!" McKinsey cried out. "Side Bar!"

From what I heard then, it was obvious things were heating up.

"This is all horseshit!" McKinsey said, "and has nothing to do with the case!"

"You were the one who bought up 'the fields,'" Zuckermann replied.

"Nevertheless, it's time to shut it all down. I'm also going to object to any testimony about Kim Worthington while in the hospital."

"Sheppard has already mentioned the two women kissing in the hospital," Zuckermann said.

"I hate that business."

The judge eyed McKinsey coldly. "Sheppard gave the 'kissing testimony' under your questioning."

"He must have snuck it in."

Zuckermann punched McKinsey lightly on his left arm. "Fred, let's put this aside for now. I would like to call one of my witnesses if you don't mind. He's already sitting in the courtroom and is ready to go. It won't take long."

"Good to go," McKinsey said. "Good to go. But then I want to get back at that Sheppard. He has information about the skinny, young gun slinger and I'm going to pry it out of him. I'm going to break his balls!" He said this as both men were walking away from the judge, who was not hearing much of anything anyway.

The judge dismissed me then, but I was told to remain ready to be recalled. I took my place behind Kim and the others and watched as Cramer was sworn in.

"You are Detective Wilson Cramer," Zuckermann began, "and you've interviewed Michael Sheppard twice, I believe, and Kim Worthington at least once."

"Affirmative to both questions."

"Michael Sheppard and Kim Worthington often drove around in a mid-sized Ford. Have you ever seen them in this car?"

"Yes, just outside the Worthington house on the east side. I had followed them there in my own cruiser."

"What was your proximity to this automobile?"

"I was knocking on the left front window. The two inside didn't know I was there."

"Were the two kissing?" Zuckermann asked, as he smirked back at McKinsey.

"No. I've never seen the two kissing."

"Explain what transpired after you knocked on the window."

"Mr. Sheppard lowered it. I told him I needed to speak with him about a Russian student named Paul Stipanovitch and that I would meet him at his house at the foot of the hill. This interview had involved the unsolved murder of Roberta Simms."

"Your witness," Zuckermann told McKinsey. McKinsey stepped forward.

"What was the exact position of the young people inside the automobile, Mr. Cramer?"

"Michael Sheppard was seated behind the wheel, Ms. Worthington had flipped around and her head was resting back against Mr. Sheppard's shoulder."

"How long did it take Sheppard to meet you down at his home?"

"Five minutes, max."

"Of course what might have transpired in that length of time is anybody's guess."

"I wouldn't know. I was no longer there."

I noticed that McKinsey was more and more unsteady on his feet. He wouldn't be able to go on much longer unless the judge called a recess.

"Mr. Cramer, what was the police interest in the Russian Student, Paul Stipanovitch?"

"At that time he was a suspect in the murder investigation of Roberta Simms. Since then, of course, the stepfather has been indicted for the crime. Strangely enough, Spitanovitch disappeared about the same time as Roberta Simms. As far as we know, he hasn't been seen in Denver since."

"I understand you had a second interview with Michael Sheppard and Kim Worthington."

"Yes, but you've already alluded to this other meeting. It was much earlier, actually on Ms. Worthington's thirteenth birthday. I was the detective who stopped by to lecture Kim and Michael about kissing in front of the picture window, and other matters relating to their friendship."

"And that's it? The subject we already discussed?"

"I'm afraid so. Not too much there to chew on. Sorry."

"No further questions," McKinsey stated with some impatience. He looked toward the judge. "I should now like to recall Michael Sheppard," he said.

I listened as the judge called me forward again. I was reminded that I was still under oath.

"Mr. Sheppard, I have heard from others that Ms. Worthington loved kisses and was drawn to blood. Would you agree?"

"Objection!" Zuckermann roared. "Hearsay!"

"Sustained. You do not need to answer that question, Mr. Sheppard." I noticed McKinsey was laughing.

"Do you remember an incident involving a scooter, and blood?"

"Yes, the accident happened…"

"Accident? I have information that Ms. Worthington admitted she had bopped herself in the nose six or eight times just to get the blood flowing that day in order to have an excuse to knock on your door and ask for help."

"Three times!" Kim yelled out. "And you're an idiot!"

"Mr. Zuckermann, please control your client!"

I noticed McKinsey was advancing toward Kim's table. He leaned down toward her face. "I'm going to see you in prison. Watch me!" I heard about this threat later.

I saw a flash of white and then McKinsey backing away, holding his nose.

"Mr. Zuckermann?" the judge asked, "did your client strike Mr. McKinsey?"

"I didn't see a thing," Your Honor. "God Almighty," he said, half under his breath.

"Do we need a recess?" Judge Simon asked McKinsey.

"No," McKinsey snarled. "Let's march on!" After hesitating a few seconds, he turned back to me.

"Mr. Sheppard, now I'm not going to ask you for a name here, but you'll remember the baseball incident. You had taken a young woman into your home."

"Roberta Simms. She is now deceased."

"Yes. Yes. Okay. Now, please relate to us what happened an hour later when you and your girlfriend came outside to your car."

But before I could answer, I saw something unbelievable. My God, I think, Kim is going for the judge! No. No. She's racing toward the rear exit now. A rather hefty guard was chasing her. No chance there. In the back of the courtroom she made a hard right, and 20 feet later, another right.

I already know what Kim is doing here. There was never going to be a jury present in this trial. She is letting the judge know she is still mentally disturbed, just as she was while shooting me on that terrible Monday.

A guard was coming toward Kim from the front now, but he's not so fast either. As he was about to grab her she used a chair as a springboard and now raced along on a table, heading toward the front. She looked like a young boy, in the middle of a track meet. McKinsey was up against a wall praying she was not after him. She gave my hand a slap on the way by, and then stopped suddenly and began throwing kisses at the judge. After three or four kisses, she obediently held out her arms in capitulation. As she was being hand-cuffed by an out-of-breath officer, a frowning judge declared a recess until 2:00 p.m.

During this break Wilson Cramer, after explaining he was un-able to stay for the afternoon session, handed me a small note. He gave me a smile and wished me well. The note said:

McKINSEY WAS EARLIER A COP. YEARS AGO GENAVISSE SHOT McKINSEY IN THE RIGHT SHOULDER BECAUSE OF WHAT HE HAD DONE TO HIS YOUNG SISTER.

Later I gave the note to Lawyer Zuckermann, who will need to dig a little deeper. This information, however, might well blow our case wide open!

When the court reconvened at 2:00 Kim was seated in her regular place, but was not only handcuffed, but shackled. Unlike the morning session the courtroom was now full. Before the first witness (myself) was called, Judge Simon spoke with Kim directly.

"Ms. Worthington, I hope you appreciate our decision to keep you immobile for a time. We couldn't allow you to race around indiscriminately." He glanced at some notes in front of him. "You will soon be 14 years old, a young lady. I feel you should give some thought to your personality. Some of the testimony we have heard in this courtroom, for example, has frankly bothered us. My advice, Ms. Worthington, is to think before you act."

I noticed Kim was nodding a little.

"Now," the judge continued, "let us recall our previous witness, Mr. Michael Sheppard."

I was again advised that I was still under oath, and McKinsey picked up where we were when Kim made her mad dash.

"Mr. Sheppard, we were discussing what happened when you and your previous girlfriend exited your house and walked toward your car."

"Yes, Kim Worthington was still standing there in my yard with her right foot on her scooter. As Roberta and I were walking toward my car Kim must have pulled a baseball from somewhere in her clothing. I opened the right-hand door for Roberta, and closed it after she was inside. As I began walking around the car, I was struck on the side of the head with a baseball."

"Excuse me, but in your opinion was young Worthington actually aiming at your head?"

"If she wasn't she was extremely lucky, because I was a moving target when it happened."

For a few seconds McKinsey was silent and I noticed a marked difference in his attitude since this morning. Perhaps Judge Simon had given him a talking to. Or perhaps the large amount of drugs he had in him earlier had finally worn off.

"Now, Mr. Sheppard, let us again consider the Monday when you drove Kim Worthington home from the hospital. I believe you testified earlier that the two of you did not enter the home together."

"Correct. Kim entered alone, just as soon as I opened the one garage door. I took my time getting her suitcase from the trunk of my car, and other items from the back seat. When I entered the second living room, Kim and Lorna Worthington were conversing. I was not a part of their conversation. I did notice, however, that Ms. Worthington had a 22 semi automatic pistol in her hand and was waving it around. I must admit I had not known that Kim had such a weapon in the house. All I knew about was a toy Luger. By then I had set the suitcase on the floor and the other items on a second sofa."

"All right, Mr. Sheppard, let's move along. How much more time elapsed before Ms. Worthington guided you into her bedroom?"

"A minute, perhaps two. She still had her 22 semi-automatic in her right hand. I mentioned this to her."

"How was she holding the weapon then?"

"She was holding it straight down. In other words, for all practical purposes, the gun was hanging loose."

"As best you can, please give us your recollection as to what was said in Ms. Worthington's bedroom."

"I mentioned again to Kim that her 22 was still loose in her right hand. She said, 'not to worry, it was okay' or some such thing."

"What else was said?"

I hesitated, wondering if I should go on. "I told Kim she should realize that I loved her in a different way than she perhaps had thought. This did not seem to sit well with Kim. For the first time, I began to worry about the loose weapon. I knew I had made a mistake when I saw the semi-automatic rise and was now pointed at my stomach."

"What were the last words you remember hearing that day?"

"Kim said, it was all really too bad, Michael, because you were always such a damned good kisser!" That was when she shot me the first time.

"And later, you learned what?"

"That I had been shot twice more."

"Yet you refuse to press charges against Kim Worthington, a young girl who now sits handcuffed and shackled directly ahead of you on the left." McKinsey glanced back toward Zuckermann. "Your witness, Sir."

Zuckermann nodded and stepped forward.

"Mr. Sheppard, when you came into the second living room what did you remember about Ms. Worthington's demeanor?"

"She was a nervous wreck. We should remember that she had been savagely beaten only a couple of weeks before, and was only dismissed from the hospital that day."

"But in spite of the fact that the weapon was, as you said, hanging loose at first, you had no fear of actually being shot?"

"No, I only thought Kim should put the weapon away."

"Did you have any last fleeting thoughts as the semi-automatic was finally pointed at your stomach?"

"Actually, yes. I thought Kim had finally lost it, and was insane at that moment. I didn't believe she knew what she was doing."

"No further questions, Your Honor." I was finally allowed to step down.

Zuckermann glanced at his notes. "I would now like to call Officer Evan Granger," he said.

I had never met this officer, who I believe arrived at Kim's home after I was shot.

I watched as this officer was sworn in.

"Officer Granger, you were one of the first to arrive at the Worthington home after the shooting, were you not?"

"Yes. The ambulance was taking Mr. Sheppard away while I

was speaking with Lorna Worthington. Mrs. Worthington might have been the person who called the authorities, though I'm not certain about this."

"What was the demeanor of Lorna Worthington when you arrived?"

"Distraught. Mr. Sheppard had just been shot in Kim Worthington's bedroom."

"Where was Kim Worthington at the time?"

"Racing through the house, screaming. I gathered she was temporarily insane."

"Objection," McKinsey stated. "You had not yet interviewed Ms. Worthington. On what basis had you decided she was insane?"

"Sustained," the judge answered. "Actually you may answer, Officer Granger. Just don't use the term 'insane.'"

"I understand, Your Honor. I was going by the sound. Eventually it took three of us to wrestle Ms. Worthington down. We did the best we could with her left arm, which was injured and still in a sling."

Zuckermann appeared to think things over. "No further questions Your Honor."

McKinsey stepped forward and mentioned to the judge that he would now like to interview Mrs. Lorna Worthington.

"Lorna Worthington to the stand please," the judge said in a steady voice.

How I wished I could get out of here. The police already had their ballistics. By now they had been all over Kim's bedroom. All that damned sex Lorna and I had could end up working against Kim's case!

I watched as Lorna was sworn in. The big question for me is whether or not she plans to lie. And for Stan Worthington it might be bad no matter which way it goes. Lorna is one of McKinsey's most important witnesses; in fact, I believe his entire case might rest right here with her testimony.

"Mrs. Worthington I should like to begin your testimony on the Friday before the fateful Monday when Michael Sheppard was shot. I believe you went out to the garage. Please tell us what happened there."

"I'm not at all certain I remember."

McKinsey stared at her. "Could it have had something to do with your BMW?"

"Objection, Your Honor. Leading the witness."

"Sustained," the judge said.

"Mrs. Worthington, please tell us what you remember about the garage."

"I don't remember anything special."

My God, I thought, she's either stoned or completely faking it.

McKinsey walked around a little, obviously frustrated. "What automobile do you usually use, Mrs. Worthington?"

"A BMW, but I haven't driven it for weeks."

"Mrs. Worthington, do you remember kissing Michael Sheppard on the Friday?"

Good Lord, I thought, this was nothing more than a shot in the dark! McKinsey knows nothing about any kiss.

"Why would I have kissed Michael?" Lorna answered. "He's only 18 years old, and half in love with Kim."

"Mrs. Worthington, is there something wrong here? I mean, are you perhaps ill today?"

"I'm often ill. And occasionally I can't remember things."

McKinsey paused. He knew he was venturing into dangerous territory. "Are you presently taking medicine for your condition, by that I mean drugs, of course."

"I often need pills."

"How many today?"

"Perhaps 14 or so. I don't exactly know."

I thought McKinsey might go for it now, asking about the exact names of the various medicines. But I was wrong.

"No further questions," he stated simply.

"No questions," Zuckermann said from his place next to Kim.

The judge dismissed Lorna Worthington and reminded her she could be recalled later. I heard McKinsey talking with the judge. He wants Stan Worthington on the stand. This is another testimony I would rather not have heard, though, of course, Stan might have additional information about Lorna's addiction. Meanwhile my eyes had followed Lorna as she walked down the center isle of the courtroom but, my God, she hadn't taken her seat in the back again, but had instead walked right out the rear exit.

Because I had been watching Lorna leaving, I hadn't seen Stan being sworn in. McKinsey was already beginning his questioning.

"Mr. Worthington, as you just witnessed, I believe your young wife was under some kind of medical assistance today. She mentioned pills. Do you have any knowledge concerning the type of medication she is presently taking?"

"Objection, Your Honor. Lorna Worthington's type of medication is no business of ours."

"Sustained," the judge said.

"Then how in hell am I to obtain information about that last witness?" McKinsey blurted out.

"Maybe she'll be more lucid next time," Zuckermann said.

"Your Honor, I believe I'm being mouse trapped here in this trial."

"Mouse trapped?" the judge repeated.

"Yes. People are ganging up on me. But let me try once again. Mr. Worthington, is your wife presently on some kind of medication?"

"Same objection," Zuckermann stated.

"No, overruled. This is so general, I'll allow it. By the way, Mr. McKinsey, I just happened to notice that Mrs. Lorna Worthington has now left the courtroom. She simply walked out the rear exit. Is this important?"

"Damn it, Your Honor, you see what I mean? Of course it's important! Could somebody get her back in here?"

The judge motioned to one of the police officers in the back of the room to take care of it.

McKinsey was totally frustrated now and I'm wondering if the judge was not about to call a recess soon. For now, though, McKinsey tried again. "Once more, Mr. Worthington, please answer my previous question."

"Yes, my wife is on some kind of medication. But I don't know the names of the individual drugs. However, what I observed here in this courtroom today is consistent with what my daughter and I often see in our own home."

I heard a small commotion in the back of the courtroom and when I glanced around I saw Lorna Worthington being led back to her place. Following this, McKinsey continued his questioning.

"Mr. Worthington, how long has Michael Sheppard been in your employment?"

"Since late last fall. I hired him to teach my daughter history, and to look after her in a general way."

"A university student? A freshman?"

"He's a published writer who has a full scholarship, and was the valedictorian of his class."

"Not too successful with his student in a social sense, however. I mean, she pumped three pieces of lead into him with remarkable consistency!"

"Objection, Your Honor. We have already admitted Kim Worthington shot Michael Sheppard. There is no reason to tie the act to history studies or babysitting."

My God, Kim's hand was high in the air now. She's disrupting the proceedings. "Your Honor, I would prefer that there be no further swearing in this courtroom. It offends me."

You little vixen! You've never been offended by swearing in your life! The judge, however took Kim's side.

"I agree with this," the judge said. "Proceed with your next question, Mr. McKinsey, but let us please all stop swearing, and avoid any further discussion of mouse traps."

"Yes, yes, Your Honor. Now Mr. Worthington, I know you were not present when the shooting occurred in your home. Still, do you have any reason to believe your daughter, Kim was mentally deranged when she shot Michael Sheppard?"

"Yes, I do. Had she not been deranged at that moment, she would never have shot Michael Sheppard."

"What about jealously?"

"Objection," Zuckermann said loudly. "Here you go again, Mr. McKinsey. With you it's either sex, jealously or maybe kisses."

"Sustained."

"No further questions," McKinsey said in a firm voice. "Since I continue to be bamboozled in regard to the individuals in this case, I will now turn to the forensic evidence in the home itself. I should like to call Huang Lee to the stand."

Well, here we go, I think. They've surely found something in that bedroom by now. I watched as Mr. Lee was sworn in.

"Mr. Lee, you are the chief forensic specialist in this county, are you not?"

"Yes."

"And did you not examine both the second living room and Kim Worthington's bedroom in the Worthington home?"

"Principally the bedroom."

"Did you meet anyone as you were traversing the lower floor?"

"Yes. Mrs. Lorna Worthington, relaxing on a sofa in the second living room."

"And what was your conversation with Mrs. Worthington?"

"There was none. She appeared to be sleeping." He hesitated. "Her mouth was actually slightly open."

McKinsey's eyes were rolling. He can't believe he's striking out again with this Worthington woman. He attempted to recover.

"What did you discover in the bedroom?"

"A great deal of blood on the floor in front of the bed. This blood came from three rounds fired into Mr. Sheppard's body from a 22 semi-automatic pistol."

"Were these three rounds fired simultaneously?"

"I believe they were. None of the rounds were fired into a body in prone position."

"And now, Mr. Lee, let us turn to the bed itself. What did you glen from it?"

"It was in a rumpled state. Ms. Kim Worthington had been attacked in 'the fields' two weeks previously and had not returned to her home until the Monday in question when she shot Michael Sheppard. No one had evidently remade the bed in all that time."

McKinsey was strolling around again, working up his nerve. I wondered if he would go for it.

"But you, Mr. Lee found no evidence to suggest that two mature adults had been bouncing around on that bed, day after day, multiple times a day, in an otherwise empty house?"

"Objection, Your Honor. The same old sex stuff. And please remember that Kim Worthington was still in the hospital during all the imaginary bouncing business, and also please remember that she's the only person on trial here."

"The objection is overruled in this instance. Mr. Lee, you may answer."

The specialist pondered for a few seconds. "No, I found no

such evidence. Also, there are nine other bedrooms in this home. Why, I might ask, would these two mythical people choose to bounce on a child's unmade rumpled bed?"

I saw a gleam in McKinsey's eye. Now he's really going for it!

"Well, Mr. Lee, let me explain it to you. This case has never been about insanity, or nervous breakdowns and the like. It has been about molestation, murder and the darkest corners of man's mind. And this goes all the way back to day one!"

"It began when a young child named Roberta Simms, then eight years old, was being molested by her own stepfather, and then later was murdered in a section of this county known as 'the fields.'"

"Objection, Your Honor. This is a totally different case? And Roberta Simms is now deceased!"

"No. Overruled. Let's allow Mr. McKinsey to continue on for a while. Also, there is linkage here with the attack on Kim Worthington later. I've recently heard that Kim's mangled form was discovered less than five feet from where the body of Roberta Simms was found."

"Thank you, Your Honor. Thank you." McKinsey took a deep breath. "By the time Roberta Simms met Michael Sheppard at age 17, she was a ruined woman, always searching for new sexual adventures. In the space of just one night, Sheppard led her into a land of fantasy, which was for her, a sexual jungle!"

Zuckermann was standing now. "Your Honor," he said, interrupting. "Might I make one small pronouncement?"

"Of course. Of course. We're all colleagues and friends here. Proceed."

"I believe it might be apropos to remember at this time that Michael Sheppard is the young man who has been shot. A victim who, by the way, is still crippled. He is not on trial here."

"Of course," McKinsey agreed. "Of course. Now, might I continue, Your Honor?" The exasperated judge only nodded.

"Well now, if the jungle was an aphrodisiac for young women, the next item made the outing 'double-edged.' Yes, remember, Your Honor, 'double-edged.'"

But Zuckermann was still standing. "I'm sorry, Your Honor, but I demand that this proceeding be halted. Otherwise, I will be forced to argue for a mistrial in this case!" This was, of course, Zuckermann on the attack! "Mr. McKinsey's tirade must not be allowed to continue!"

The judge leaned forward and, with his left hand cupped behind his left ear, asked Zuckermann to explain his concerns.

"I most certainly will, Your Honor. The relationship of Michael Sheppard and Roberta Simms is old history and has absolutely nothing to do with our present case. Roberta Simms has been deceased for many weeks, and Michael Sheppard had nothing to do with her death."

"But the connection with the two attacks in 'the fields' the judge countered... For example, the proximity of the two victims."

"Yes, yes, Your Honor, you are correct, but the man who committed both of these attacks is presently behind bars, awaiting trial. In my opinion, we might as well forget about 'the fields,' because what happened there had little to do with our present case. The only connection might be the effect of the attack on Kim Worthington's mental health. That should surely be considered. Kim Worthington was beaten within an inch of her life, and it was Michael Sheppard alone who saved her that night."

"Anything further?" the judge asked.

"Yes, Your Honor. There is more history at play here." Zuckermann glanced at his notes. "Several years ago a 14-year-old girl in this area was seduced by an officer of the law. He was shot afterward by another officer in revenge. Actually in the right shoulder."

"Let's stop this now!" the judge said. "It appears you are teasing those of us in this courtroom, Mr. Zuckermann. I demand additional information."

"Are you quite certain you want more information, judge? Why don't we approach Fred McKinsey about this? Of course, I could also recall Officer Wilson Cramer and put him under oath again. He knows this history well. And then, naturally I might just demand that Mr. McKinsey remove his shirt and allow us all to examine his right shoulder. How about it, Fred?"

The courtroom has exploded. The judge was pounding with his gavel and calling for order, but there was no order. Many in the courtroom were howling for McKinsey to remove his shirt. Finally McKinsey raised both his arms high. Then, after a time, order was restored.

"Whatever," McKinsey said. "Whatever you want." Now it was deathly quiet in the courtroom. Then the lawyer spoke out in a firm voice. "I wish to have nothing more to do with this case," he stated. "The case of the shackled, skinny gun slinger!" He threw up his hands again and then walked directly down the center isle and out the rear exit. He must have been hoping against hope that none of the men in the room grabbed him on the way out!

The judge looked out on the stunned and silent courtroom. He seemed to consider the situation for a minute or two. He slowly rubbed his chin. "I will need to speak with the district attorney again before we reconvene," he said. "Court is adjourned!"

In a way I was sorry to see McKinsey go, for I had a question for him. I had not understood what he meant when he referred to something as being 'double-edged.' I had never grasped this. I finally decided it was just part of his rambling.

Two days later a small announcement appeared in *The Denver Mountain Guardian*. It concerned an assistant district attorney, Fred

McKinsey, who had resigned his position in Denver to take a new position as a teacher of English in a remote girl's school in Tahiti. I imagine few people bothered to read the article.

The very next day I received a letter baring a postmark from St. Petersburg, Russia from Paul Stipanovitch. I opened it immediately. The principal news was that, being broke in Denver, he had returned to Russia and soon made peace with his previous girlfriend. They are to be married next month. He apologized for not touching base with me before leaving the United States. That was about it.

I sat there on my sofa for a while with the letter in my hand. What a problem Paul had been for many here in Denver. As things turned out, I doubt if he even knew that Roberta had been killed, nor that he was, for a time, under suspicion for her murder. How strange it had seemed when he and Roberta disappeared at about the same time. No one had been able to explain this until now. Obviously, Paul had simply gone back to Russia.

Next Monday we were to return to court to hear Judge Simon's decision about Kim. The district attorney had evidently decided we had spent enough time with this trial and that Kim's fate was now in the hands of the judge. Although the D.A. was planning to make a few remarks himself, I'm certain Zuckermann will also make a special plea to the judge regarding Kim's horrible experience in 'the fields' that night when she almost died.

Once we had assembled in the courtroom, the district attorney came by, introduced himself, and asked me once again if I was certain I did not wish to press charges against Kim Worthington (who was actually sitting next to me). I told him I did not.

The district attorney spoke first. "I have studied the transcript of this very strange trial thoroughly and have come to a few conclusions. First of all, I have no interest in birthday kisses nor the positioning of young teenagers in their cars. I have instead concentrated on Kim Worthington's shooting of Michael Sheppard on the fateful

Monday in question and her general psychological makeup. I am also cognizant of the fact that Ms. Worthington was brutally attacked in an area of our county known as 'the fields' a few weeks ago. I am certain Mr. Zuckermann will mention this fact in his closing statement." The D.A. glanced back at Zuckermann. "The time is yours, my friend."

Zuckermann stepped forward, turned and glanced around the courtroom, which at present was not even a third full. I actually believe this is all a charade, anyway, because I have a suspicion Kim's fate had already been decided behind closed doors. Still, Zuckermann went through the motions.

"Your Honor, Mr. District Attorney, Michael Sheppard and guests of the court." He paused. "To be brief, our case began when Roberta Simms, a friend of Michael Sheppard, was found murdered in a park not far from our university. Ms. Simms had been missing for quite some time and it was only when Kim Worthington discovered her body while returning from school that the case came to the quick attention of the police. Some days later Ms. Worthington herself was brutally attacked by the same murderer in the same location. This man, Roberta's stepfather, is presently in custody awaiting his own trial for committing these crimes."

"We the defense have always admitted that Kim Worthington shot Michael Sheppard, almost certainly because of a disagreement regarding their young relationship. But now, as I close my remarks, I wish to plead for leniency in this case. Kim Worthington is an A student. Michael Sheppard, one of her teachers, has asked the prosecution not to press charges against her. Ms. Worthington received great trauma when she discovered Roberta's body all alone while walking in 'the fields.' Again, as stated earlier, she herself was attacked and nearly died, saved only by Michael Sheppard, who carried her to safety. Because of this recent history, Your Honor, I plead for leniency this morning. Thank you."

Judge Simon glanced at Kim. "Ms. Worthington, would you please rise for sentencing." Kim stood straight and tall, her hands folded in front of her. As I was seated on her left, I quickly touched my right leg gently against her knee in moral support. She smiled a little then.

"Ms. Worthington, you are not going to prison. Instead I am sentencing you to nine months in a mental facility called Brook Farm, a beautiful park-like place near the South Platte River. I wish to emphasize that this sentence is flexible. If you are helpful to others in this facility, and if you can persuade the authorities there that you have improved psychologically in terms of anger management, you might be released earlier. I wish to emphasize that some in this establishment could really use your help. In other words, some there are in far worse shape than yourself. You will notice this immediately. During this space of time your education will continue. Michael Sheppard has agreed to continue as your history teacher and, of course, books will be provided as needed. But you will also be expected to be helpful in this home. That is part of your sentence. I have every confidence that you will succeed there. I am giving you two days to prepare for your new home. They will be expecting you in the middle of the afternoon on the second day. I wish you luck, Ms. Worthington." The judge scanned the courtroom then, perhaps to make certain all was in order there. After glancing once more at Kim, he declared the court was adjourned.

We all shook hands with Zuckermann, thanking him for his support, but as we left the courthouse I was already smiling to myself. So, I thought, the judge had patiently listened to the brief remarks of both the district attorney and lawyer Ben Zuckermann, after which time he ignored both men and abruptly sentenced Kim to nine months in a mental institution. It was all preordained, just as I had thought, with Stan's money smoothing every obstacle along the way. By then I was laughing out loud. I just couldn't help myself.

Except for Kim being sentenced to a home for the mentally ill (I choked because I was laughing so hard) everything else was running smoothly. Lorna had not visited me again and she and Stan seemed happier than I had ever seen them. I am taking a couple of summer courses and so far am keeping up with the work. In a few weeks my parents will be returning home from Hawaii and it almost pains me when I consider having to share all the negative aspects of my life since they've been gone.

On Sunday afternoon around 2:00, Kim, Stan, Lorna and myself loaded into the large Mercedes and drove southwest toward the mental facility on the South Platte. Kim's demeanor was good and she seemed interested in the idea of a new life. Her three suitcases were in the trunk.

As we approached the home, the size of the place made a strong impression on me. The grounds themselves stretched on seemingly forever. I can imagine a person getting lost on some of the paths. We soon learned that Kim had a single room on the second floor and, after unloading the suitcases there, we returned to meet with a young woman, perhaps 30 years old, named Ms. Catlack, in an office not far from the large main door which we had entered earlier. There were many people milling about, both inside and out on the grounds. I must confess I haven't seen any actual lunatics yet, at least none I could identify.

Following introductions Ms. Catlack explained that, although Kim would be encouraged to continue her studies, she would also be expected to work.

"Whose job will it be to keep track of me here?" Kim asked.

"Do you feel you need such a person? We're sort of in a wilderness area here."

"I've already noticed the trees along the South Platte River, which runs northeast back through Denver and then, with the North Platte, hits the Missouri River somewhere south of Omaha. The Platte back to Denver might be a nice walk." Everybody knew Kim was kidding. "Besides studying," she continued, "what would I be doing to help you here?"

Ms. Catlack nodded. "You will have six students in the beginning. They are somewhat handicapped. They can sing. They can dance. They love doing that. They are, however, somewhat slow as regards basic learning. A girl like you should be able to help them a lot. Your goal should be to make them self-sufficient as much as possible. They need to be able to handle money in a store or a gas station. In other words, they should be able to add and subtract. Don't worry about fractions." Ms. Catlack smiled. "They will all regard you as their teacher. They will respect you. They will listen to you."

"When should I be up in the morning? What time is breakfast? What about my first class?"

"Breakfast is from eight until nine. Let's have you meet your class from 10:00 to 11:30. Your class will not meet on the weekends. Also, you won't need to chaperone these students at lunch. After lunch feel free to take a walk, or work on your studies. And again, no one will be watching you. You're on your own."

Kim nodded pleasantly. "Thank you very much."

"Why don't you and your family take a walk around the grounds?" Catlack suggested.

We certainly all agreed with this and walked out the same door from which we had entered earlier. "It's a piece of cake," I said lightly as we strolled along. Although I was limping just a little, it really didn't bother me much as long as the others didn't go too fast. "They've done research on you, Kim," I continued. "They know how smart you are."

"Maybe," Kim said. "The teaching sounds interesting."

"They all know the other 'mental stuff' was a fake," Stan said. "They let us get away with it because they didn't want to deal with a prison sentence."

Lorna glanced at Kim. "It seems they've sent you here just to teach six kids. As Michael said, 'a piece of cake.'"

Meanwhile I was watching some of the others who were walking along. Some were older and could perhaps be parents. Soon I would need to find out the total make up of people in this home. Ms. Catlack had not mentioned any sort of danger. I wondered if things could really be that safe here.

"When one looks at this home carefully," Lorna said, "One soon realizes it's a huge structure. Look up ahead, there's a complete other wing off to the right. There must be hundreds staying here."

Kim and I had been walking along together. Stan leaned forward and touched Kim on her right shoulder. "I'm amazed at the freedom you have here, Kim. It's not what I expected. Surely this can't be true for everyone."

"Agreed," Kim said. "And there could be some troublemakers around. I saw there's a lock on my door. At night I'm going to use it."

"I noticed your nice bathroom and shower," Lorna said. "You're getting special treatment, Kim. There's no way they can give others a deal like this."

As we strolled along I was looking over the various paths. Some ran at a diagonal, and one ran directly toward the trees along the South Platte River. Although we met people along the way, our stroll was not at all crowded. Suddenly I took Kim's arm and stopped us. I had seen a man who was walking left at a diagonal away from us. A young woman was on his right holding onto his arm. I know this man. He is Officer Lester Genavissie, who had met me at my home the morning after Kim was attacked in 'the fields.' He had been totally unfriendly and had ordered me held in the police station for hours later that same day. Oddly enough, this was the officer who had shot Fred McKinsey in the right shoulder in revenge for him seducing his young sister, the act that had blown Kim's trial wide open. Although Zuckermann had mentioned Genavissie in our pre-trial practice session, his name never came up in the trial itself. I doubt anyone walking with me now remembered it.

"I have additional information about the home here," Stan said suddenly. It would be possible for the three of us to have lunch with Kim on Sundays."

"Wonderful," Lorna said. "Let's do it." Kim and I nodded in agreement. Little by little we drifted back toward the area of our car. Kim didn't seem bothered by us leaving. As we prepared to say good-bye Lorna asked Kim if she had any last minute concerns.

"Just that it all seems unbelievable. I shot my boyfriend three times, ruining his left leg forever, and I'm sentenced to having a private room in a nice large home, and teaching six kids for an hour and a half, five days a week. No wonder people keep breaking the law. There doesn't seem to be much of a down side to it."

I smiled. "I'll be back Tuesday afternoon," I told her. We all hugged each other then and Kim waved goodbye.

The conversation back to Denver was totally positive, with everyone, including myself, remarking about Kim's situation in the home. Stan reiterated what he had said during our walk earlier, that most people suspected Kim had been faking the mental stuff, and simply overlooked it for one reason or another. He also mentioned that another factor was that I had refused to press charges. Lorna was naturally sitting in the front seat close to Stan. I can't help wondering if she ever thinks of me. Surely she does. I'm certainly glad the two of them appear happy.

Back in my own home at the foot of the hill I was struck by the fact that Kim was no longer living in the big home at the top. Of course, physically I had known this, but psychologically, especially after a while when I walked out on my porch and glanced up toward the left, it hit me. I was also somewhat lonely. Kim was on the South Platte, and Lorna was evidently not planning to visit me alone for a while.

When loneliness strikes it's time to hit the books! At least that had been my philosophy up to this point in my life. One of my classes here in the late summer dealt with the years leading up to the French Revolution, the other with the poetry of Pushkin. Yes, back to young Tatianna again. Perhaps her memory might be a comfort to me now.

While reading the French history text I noticed my mind continued to wander. It was not Kim I was thinking of then, but rather an officer of the law named Lester Genavissie. What was he doing, walking around in that mental health institution? But then I thought of the younger woman who was holding onto his right arm. Could she have been his sister? Could she be the one living in the home, perhaps even now negatively affected by her prior relationship with Fred McKinsey from so many years ago?

I will never learn the answers to these questions without touching base with a couple of my acquaintances in the police station, namely Cramer and/or Wonderlich. I'm actually not concerned about Genavissie in terms of my own safety. I'm thinking about Kim. If the man is unbalanced, God knows what he might do. I plan to get on this problem in the morning.

At present I have my French history book in bed. I'll continue reading it there until I fall asleep. Twenty minutes later I laid the book aside and grabbed a pillow. And who will be joining me tonight as I sleep? Probably the dreamy beautiful girl from New Orleans who had worked her will on me and led me into a bedroom I should never have visited, facing a 22 semi-automatic pistol which I had no idea was even present in the house. Actually, that night I dreamed about a Russian man named Eugene, who seemed to be trying to locate a young girl named Tatianna. It was a mixed up affair, which did not end well for Eugene Onegin.

On Monday morning, after returning home from my French History class, I called Detective Wilson Cramer in the police station and casually mentioned that I had seen Officer Lester Genavissie walking along in the grounds of the large mental health facility where my friend Kim was staying. I explained further: "Because Genavissie had been so negative toward me from the first day we met, I'm naturally interested in his whereabouts."

A long pause followed while Cramer no doubt considered whether he should be discussing Genavissie with me at all.

"You'll surely remember the story of the young sister," he said finally. "Could a female have been accompanying him there in the park? Of course, you might also speak with people in the home itself. Perhaps they might be able to provide you with a small amount of information. I can tell you that Officer Genavisse is not well. Of course, I don't know any of the particulars."

"I'm glad you brought up the sister. There was a younger woman walking with him yesterday."

"Another person you might chat with is Detective Wonderlich. Because he's getting close to retirement, he occasionally visits with other officers who have personal problems." Cramer paused. "Speaking of problems, how is your friend, Kim getting along? She has a private room perhaps? A sweet deal generally?" I heard Cramer laughing. I knew he was thinking of Stan's money.

"Kim is teaching six students there in the home. She doesn't have a heavy load."

"Ah, not a heavy load. Interesting." He laughed again. "What about Stipanovitch? Ever hear from him? Not that it matters much now."

"He's back in Russia. Back with his previous girlfriend. Things turned out okay. Well, Detective, thanks a lot. I may give Detective Wonderlich a call later."

"Good idea. He might have more information about Genavisse. Take care, Michael."

"So long, Detective." I wondered if I would ever see him again.

Stepping back out on my porch I looked up toward Kim's home, and then stared across the road toward 'the fields.' It was now late morning. And would you go into that place again without the Glock, I asked myself. No, probably not. Too much had happened there. Perhaps this was just a psychological weakness on my part. But the fact remained. Not without the Glock.

I glanced at my yard and saw the grass was getting higher on the east side. I decided to go to the garage and take out my little push mower. I can easily knock out this section of the yard right now. I rolled out the mower. As usual, each time I turned to take another strip of grass I glanced up the hill toward Kim's large home. I soon saw someone walking toward me. It was Lorna. I stopped mowing and waited for her.

"You don't happen to have a baseball on you, do you? Kim and I often played catch here."

"I throw a ball like a six year old. Not like your spitfire, who can knock you out with her fast ball."

We gazed at each other. I took a deep breath. "That first evening I told you I would never love you. It turned out to be an untruth. I wanted you to know this, Lorna."

"I feel the same toward you, Michael." She laughed. "Maybe we should think about running for it—New Orleans, or another place."

"And rob banks or something for money, like Bonnie and Clyde? These people usually ended up badly. Come on, Lorna, let's sit together on my porch steps. I'll grab a couple of Cokes." I already knew Lorna had no interest in this plan. I came back with the pop, opened hers and winked at her. I opened my Coke and then we touched our cans together in a toast.

"I can't believe we're sitting here on your front steps drinking Coke."

I paused. "I need to talk with you Lorna. Whatever happens, we have to remain best friends. But we have a problem. Kim has already given us a prelude of what we could be facing down the line."

"So, what's the message?" She hesitated, waiting for my reply. When I didn't answer immediately, she continued. "You pressured me into keeping Stan happy. Well, I've become one of the biggest fakers in the history of the world. And Stan is happy as a clam!"

"But I guess you still don't know if you love him."

"You idiot! You know who I love. Now listen, I'm willing to be cagey, but not today. It has been too long. Kim is out of the way, and Stan is in Boulder working with a real estate deal. What more do you want, young student?"

I grinned at her. "Let's finish our pop first. You know, maybe think things over."

"You're treating me like Kim. Keeping me here outside on the steps."

I laughed. "Oh, come on, then. Bring your pop with you. We'll go in."

Half an hour later Lorna was sobbing, completely out of control. I continued kissing her softly and telling her I loved her. Minutes later she began sort of choking and gagging, like on a bone.

"What are we going to do about Kim?" she asked, touching her throat and coughing a little more.

"Oh, that will work out, one way or another. But I won't give in to her, Lorna. We're a long way from the 19th century. Some in the police force take their jobs more seriously these days. I keep telling Kim she needs a boyfriend two years younger than me."

"That's a laugh." Lorna coughed again. "Kim will never give you up. She's like that young Russian girl. I've heard her talk about this. And you're seeing her tomorrow afternoon?"

"Yes, that's the plan."

"Why do you like this bean pole?"

"I don't know. I just do." I hesitated. "But please, forget about Kim. We need to concentrate on our safety. Do you think Stan has ever suspected?"

"No. I doubt it. As far as I know he has complete faith in you."

"How's your battle with the pills? Are you giving them up, little by little?"

"I've given them up completely. I knew you wanted this for me. I, too, am happy as a clam. Love conquers all."

"I'm glad to see you today. I thought maybe you'd given me up."

"No you didn't. You knew damned well I would be back. Good God, how could you doubt it?"

I grinned at her. "What if I told you some people might suggest we're being selfish? Risking the destruction of an entire family because of our satisfaction in bed. That's why I suggested we sit outside and drink pop. By the way, I'm considering myself a part of this family."

She stared at me. "You're asking me to give up an important part of my life."

"I understand, but Lorna, will you at least give my previous idea some thought? I mean, us just being friends?"

"Sure. I can consider anything. But one can always keep kicking the goddamned can down the road, too." She was already dressing to leave.

And should you visit me again, I thought, I will make certain all you receive at my house is a cold can of pop! But I smiled at her as she was leaving.

I arrived at the large institution on the South Platte about 2:00 on Tuesday, but instead of looking for Kim immediately, I went to the main office first and asked for information about Lester Genavissie. I told the woman there I had known him earlier as a police officer. Although she wasn't willing to provide many facts, I did learn that it was Genavisse himself who was living in the home, not his daughter. This was at least a start.

I found Kim in her room. She begged me to cancel our history lesson and instead accompany her on a long walk.

"And would your father approve of this?" I asked, laughing a little.

"He doesn't care what we do. Come on. Let's go!"

It was a beautiful summer day and I was glad to be outside strolling myself. "How has the teaching been going, Kim? Any problems so far?"

"No, I love it. I could do it forever. My students are not terribly bright, of course, but they try so hard it's a pleasure to be with them."

"Good Lord, Kim, I've never seen you so happy!"

"You're right, I'm content here." She whispered then. "Nothing like a 'nut house' to bring out the best in a person." She laughed. "Come on, let's head for the Platte River. I want to see how big it is."

"You may find it rather small at this juncture." I smiled at her.

We were walking at a moderate pace because Kim knew that speed was my enemy as far as my left knee was concerned. We had been strolling hand in hand, though I doubt anybody cared.

"Kim!" I said, what finally happened to that paper you wrote about the Salem witches?"

"I received an A on it and then heaved the whole thing. After shooting you it was too easy to identify with a couple of the witches."

"I understand." We continued our walk.

As we approached the South Platte we appeared to be alone on this path, and we were a long way from the home itself. Suddenly Kim stopped me. We could both see the river through the trees. "Pretend it's my birthday," she said. "There's no one around."

I took a good look to the right and the left, then I finally nodded and took her in my arms and kissed her. I hope it made her happy. We turned then and made our way back to the large home. By then, however, I was no longer thinking about Kim. I knew sometime tomorrow I would be calling Detective Wonderlich about Genavisse.

The next morning after my class I called Wonderlich and asked if he had 10 minutes or so. He suggested I come on ahead.

"Cramer told me you've been worried about Officer Genavissie," he said when meeting me at the station.

I gazed at him seriously and shrugged.

"Your young friend, Kim can fake mental illness. Genavissie really is ill! This man has deteriorated even more in the past few weeks. I believe Cramer told you, because I'm nearing retirement, I'm sometimes given the chance to visit with retired officers who have problems. I met with Genavissie Monday afternoon for half an hour."

"I know about his daughter."

"Yes, and she's a great help. She visits him every couple of days. This man is no danger to you, Mr. Sheppard. Just forget about him."

The Detective's cell phone rang. "Hang on a minute," he told me. I listened quietly. I saw his right hand clutch the phone tighter. "When did it happen? You're certain it was the wife? I suppose it shouldn't surprise me. No, I'll come right over. Maybe 10 minutes." He snapped his cell shut and stared at me.

"Lawyer Ben Zuckermann's dead. His wife caught him in bed with his blonde secretary. The wife evidently kept squeezing the trigger of her 45 automatic until it jammed. I naturally have to leave. I've known the wife and her husband for years."

"Of course. Rather active, wasn't he? Begged his wife to take him back when returning from Barbados and then jumped right into bed with his ex-secretary again. Some men just wear themselves out, and then they die." I raised my hand in farewell.

"So long, Detective. It's been grand!"

The funeral for Ben Zuckermann was a great affair for the masses, though not for me. He was a fine lawyer, but the two of us had never been close, principally because of certain lies he had formulated about Kim, her stepmother and Stan. Also, I never thought he liked me much, suggesting he found it strange that certain women seemed to gravitate toward me. I guess he thought that was his area of expertise.

The following Sunday Lorna, Stan and I loaded into the Mercedes again and drove to the mental health facility to have lunch with Kim who, as far as we knew, was still content teaching her six students. Meanwhile my mind was wandering.

Once, when I was a small child, an elderly man who lived near us used to sing a crazy song about being in jail. I'm certain I could still sing the melody. Anyway, as Stan, Lorna and I walked toward the institution to have lunch, I could not get that old tune out of my mind. Of course, what was really on my mind now was: 'I'm in the nut house now; I'm in the nut house now.' This was, of course, totally unfair. This home is basically a beautiful place and with all the interesting paths available for strolling, plus the large number of friendly help, no one should ever be complaining.

Thinking we would probably be having lunch in the commons room, I was amazed when we were led into a specious private dining room with the table set for four. Kim had already joined us. After making our choices for lunch, Kim led a discussion, which she remembered from one of my own lessons. It concerned Poland and the labor unions that had fought against the communists in the last decades of the 20th century, with help from the Polish Pope, John Paul. She remembered the word, SOLIDARITY and somehow connected this word to our present family.

"That battle reminds me of our family," she said. "All four of us. So, yes, let's chant the word a little while waiting for our food. Come on, let's go!"

And so, here it came, the Polish battle cry now connected to our own family. SOLIDARITY, SOLIDARITY, SOLIDARITY. Kim's face was beaming. "That was just great," she said. I too had mouthed the words, though what I was really contemplating while glancing around the table, was: 'I wonder what in hell I'm going to do with these two young females, as I proceed with my life, the two who seem so attached to me. I know I have problems in this regard. Naturally I should be tougher. I should lay down the law.

But that's not so easy either.

This became evident that last day when Lorna walked down the hill and I suggested we sit outside on my steps and drink Coke. How quickly I gave in. There seems to be some kind of mechanism in my mind. It began a long time ago, on the day of Kim's 13th birthday when I first kissed her on the forehead thinking it would be enough to please her.

'Baby kiss' she had said. Well, naturally I soon stepped for-ward and kissed her full on the mouth. I've probably loved her from that moment forward. But the problem remains in my life. My God, I've already been shot three times! Yet I always remain on the side of the females. I'm locked in. For you see, I just can't stand breaking their hearts!

I continued seeing Kim twice a week for our history lesson, mostly Tuesday and Thursday and, in spite of our many studies, we often took time out for walks along the various beautiful paths. Kim continued to be happy with her teaching and the four of us had lunch every Sunday in our special dining room reserved just for us.

Two months into Kim's servitude she and her father were called before a small board of four to discuss the possibility of Kim leaving the home much earlier than had been anticipated (something I learned only later, second hand). This was due to her constant im-provement as far as anger management was concerned, and the praise she received from teaching her small class of six students. The board took only five minutes to make a decision.

Kim's hand was immediately in the air, however. "There is something the four of you should remember. In the 60 days I've been here in this place not one of you has discussed my mental health personally. Only Dr. Silverstein continued to meet with me. For all the four of you know, I might still be crazy as a bed bug."

"You know, the only reason I wasn't sent to prison originally was because Michael Sheppard refused to press charges against me. That's why the four of you were finally stuck with me. Still, you re-fused to take me seriously. We can only hope you haven't made a mistake."

When I read this account later, I was convinced Kim had felt guilty for being released so soon. Having shot me three times she felt she deserved a much longer sentence.

In following the report, Ms. Catlack, who was a member of

the board, stated: "I've read Dr. Silverstein's reports and frankly I agree with him. I can't see there is anything wrong with you."

"Your attitude probably reflects my recent history, which means you have no knowledge of what I was up to before."

"Before is not our concern," Charles Wade, another member of the board, said. "Past history is none of our business."

"Let's remember one thing," Kim fired back. "I was sentenced to this home for shooting the young man I love three times, once in the left leg which almost crippled him."

"You should take this up with the judge who sentenced you," Stacy O'Conner said. O'Conner was a third member of the board.

"Fine," Kim said quietly. "Then perhaps I can vacate my room sometime today."

Stan Worthington spoke up then for the first time. "We can vacate Kim's room within 10 minutes," he said.

"Sounds great," Christina Romer said. "Ms. Worthington, just to make things clear, this is a mental health facility. We can't allow perfectly sane people to hang around indefinitely on the public dole. Others are waiting for a space."

Kim glanced at her father and the two of them went upstairs to pack her things.

And so, being banished from the institution after serving a scant two months, Kim was transported back to her home on the hill, where she continued to mingle with Lorna, her father and naturally myself.

Meanwhile, an entire year had passed. The four of us were soon to celebrate Kim's 14th birthday. Her personality had remained steady and I would have to admit was much improved. She was also studying French with a passion, insisting no Parisian would ever confuse her with any claptrap American tourist strolling nearby.

She was naturally also changing physically and very soon she would no longer be able to place her hands against her flat chest and pronounce that 'had she had tits she would already be out there conquering the world.' Well, soon she'll have them and we'll see.

A week after we celebrated Kim's birthday my parents returned from Hawaii. I quickly shared the news of the large events—Roberta's murder and my continued success in the university, but I left out Kim's violence and, of course, Lorna's seduction of me. Although I had never suggested a social meeting between my parents and the Worthington family, as soon as Kim realized my parents were home, she set up a Sunday afternoon get-together. No one ever mentioned Lorna's age or that she was a stepmother, although I doubt either of my parents believed she was Kim's actual mother. And as for Kim, well, she was a perfect young angel, therefore it was a nice afternoon all the way around.

I believe it was my father sometime during the first days he was back who remarked, "What are you doing teaching the young kid? She seems so proper your mother and I wondered if she might not be planning to enter a convent."

"Could be," I said, without another word. I could scarcely keep myself from laughing out loud.

There are, of course, other positive factors in my life. Although Lorna visited me more than once at my home, all she ever received from me was a cold can of pop while sitting on my front steps. When she finally realized what was happening to our relationship, she refused to speak to me for almost two weeks.

I hated this, but it seemed to be the only way I could get myself to break it off with her. I continued to remind myself that our physical relationship had been her idea from the beginning and that, as the old saying went, 'she had known what the job was when she signed on for it.' Still, I continued to miss her profoundly. I just didn't show it. Of course, I felt a lot better in regard to my friend, Stan Worthington, though I doubt I'll ever forgive myself for what I had done with Lorna on the sly.

Kim, of course, being 14, is already a freshman in high school. As I remembered back over the past year I was proud to say I had never placed the slightest pressure on her as regards our friendship. Had she come to me one day with a young man on her arm, complete with introductions, I would have smiled broadly and not interfered with her plans whatsoever. Of course, I had warned her more than once about trying to continue a relationship with an 18-year-old. It was a constant struggle.

Lorna, meanwhile, seemed so determined to get me back, one way or another, I've become afraid she might do something to Kim to get her out of the way. This was the reason I had taken action 30 minutes ago when I lifted the 22 semi-automatic from the shoebox under Kim's bed and waltzed it down the hill to my own home and locked it away securely. I'm obviously becoming paranoid.

While returning from a Saturday afternoon jaunt to the mall, Kim, who was more and more often making decisions about the large home, decided to settle a few questions in advance. "First of all, I want no one calling me while I'm in school. Talk to me after I'm home in the afternoon. And know one thing for certain, I don't give a ding-dong about what goes on in this house while I'm away. I'm talking now about the two of you." (She was pointing at Lorna and me).

"And Lorna, you may have noticed that Michael and I have not been going out much together. The police already have their damned eye on us. I want the police to forget we exist."

"Now on another matter, Lorna. I've loved you from that first day forward, but I've always thought you resented me, in fact, feared me a little. How do you plan to deal with this?"

Lorna hesitated. "I've always thought you were too young for Michael. I did not agree with my husband when he put Michael in charge of you most afternoons. Granted, you learned a lot of history, but all the physical affection stuff beginning at the age of 12 was pure nonsense, asking for trouble."

"You were building that relationship up in your mind," Kim said. "Michael didn't even kiss me until age 13 on my birthday. The question is, what do you plan to do about me now?"

"I doubt if I can do anything. We're both in love with the same young man and you'll probably win because you'll be the one who eventually wants the babies. Your only problem is the police. Of course, maybe the two of us will wear Michael out and he'll simply run for the hills!"

I pulled into the garage area on the big east side. "Good Lord, ladies, you're making me feel like a damned piece of meat, available to the highest bidder."

In the house Kim continued her conversation with Lorna in the second living room. "As I said before, I've always had the greatest affection for you, Lorna from the very first day you came to us. But you appear somewhat uncertain about things now. Why don't you share your thoughts with us?"

Lorna hesitated a moment. "Everything appears to be in a muddle. I keep thinking back to that terrible Monday, the day Michael was shot. There are too many emotions floating around in this house."

"Too many emotions, huh? Well, I rather agree with you on that score, Lorna. For example, what's your fascination with my bedroom? Why did you need to fuck Michael there? You took him in my bedroom twice. I think you owe me, Lorna. I'm feeling the need for a little revenge! We're exactly the same size, you know. Why I'll bet I could just take you down, sit on you and then start tickling you half to death." Kim was grinning.

"Michael? Help me here. Don't let her."

"Kim, let's not have any tickling. Okay?"

"All right. However, I do need something. My revenge, you

know." Kim stood and walked up to Lorna who was standing herself then. "Just remain calm, Lorna. Don't worry about a thing." Kim was holding Lorna by her upper arms, but then she gently folded Lorna in against her and kissed her on the mouth for a long time.

"Kim, come on now. Settle down! Enough!"

"Okay, okay," Kim said. She gently eased herself away from Lorna.

I threw up my arms and sat down on one of the sofas. Lorna rushed over and sat close to me, grabbing for my hand. Kim was looking at her.

"Let me tell you something, Lorna, before I forget it. That sweet little mouth of yours should be banned by the government! I'm still dizzy from your kiss! Stay away from her, Michael. Kiss her, and you'll be running your car into a ditch!"

"But, Lorna, I think you need to toughen up," Kim said, continuing. "Bite the bullet as they say. And speaking of bullets, yesterday I found that my 22 semi-automatic is now missing from the shoebox under my bed. Michael no doubt has spirited it away down the hill to his own house. Ah, sharing."

"But, Lorna, with all the sharing going on around us, it might be better to just pretend we're running a whore house here. You're from New Orleans; you've surely heard of such things. And we should all be tolerant. Should one hear raucous shrieks being emitted from various rooms in this great mansion, well that should not detract us from the joys of our daily lives. Actually, screaming with a man in bed is good for strengthening a woman's lungs. I assure you, Lorna, sometime in the future I plan to scream bloody murder!" Kim laughed. She was reminding me about my telling her stories about Lorna's screaming in bed, information which I should definitely not have shared.

"Don't you think perhaps the three of us are destined to hell because of your 'whore house' analogy coming to light?" Lorna asked.

"I doubt it, but if you were so worried about such things why did you seduce my boyfriend while committing adultery yourself? This was while I was lying helpless in bed in the hospital."

"I had special problems."

"So did my father, and for months you did nothing to support him."

"You think I'm lucking out with the inheritance money, don't you?"

"Actually yes, that's what I think." Kim paused for a second or two. "But please remember, Lorna, Michael Sheppard was my boyfriend first. Right now he's just on loan to you. You surely can't think you'll be able to hold him."

My God, I was thinking, I'm in more trouble than I knew. Kim evidently believes I'm still sleeping with Lorna.

Kim hesitated and then looked us both in the eye. "Michael ultimately belongs to me, and I'm grabbing him back just as soon as the law allows it!"

Watching Kim's face I found it nondescript, a face no stranger could ever read. From the corner of my right eye I saw Lorna Worthington shudder slightly. Lorna stood then and walked away, maybe going to her own bedroom this time, a place I've never visited.

"What did you think of my little speech?" Kim asked me.

"One of your worst. I hated it."

"It was for the benefit of 'play mother.' By the way, she any good in bed?"

"Come on, Kim. Let it rest. And actually, you're way off base here. I haven't been intimate with Lorna since the days you were trapped in that institution on the South Platte."

"Glad to hear it. It was about time you shaped up." She grinned at me. "Any new ideas about why she hustled you into my own bedroom earlier?"

I shook my head. "Look, I know you love her, and I know

she's scared of you. Beyond that I'm at a loss. I know one thing though, your 'play mother' is one strange lady. I suggest we let all this rest."

"Okay," Kim paused for several seconds. "Are you up on the plans for France?"

I gave her a puzzled look. "I know you've been studying the language like a mad woman. Your French teacher told me recently he's certain you're a genius."

"The genius bit is a result of a whole lot of hard work. But you know nothing about any future vacation plans?"

"Guess not. Why haven't you been keeping me up-to-date?"

"Oh, high school and everything, I don't know. Actually, father is not just considering France, he wants us to visit most of Europe. A six- or seven-week tour."

I smiled. "I guess he's eventually planning to discuss this project with me."

"I suppose so." Kim was pondering. "I'd like to start out with Italy. This could be in the late winter, or very early spring, of course."

"Naturally. And then?"

"Oh, north through the Brenner Pass, into Austria and Germany." She saw I was staring at her. "Come on, Michael, we both know you've taught me well. Of course, I'm up on the geography." She hesitated. "I'd like to spend at least a week in Munich, and another week in Prague."

"And since we are already traveling in a northeasterly direction, why not hit Krakow for a couple of days, followed by St. Petersburg? Maybe look up Paul Stipanovitch and his new wife there?"

"Not a chance! I've never trusted that man! But your idea about St. Petersburg in general is great! Definitely need a week in the old city of the Czars."

"And then, Kim, how about a few days in England?"

"Yes! It will be our next to the last stop. Elizabeth Tower, the

Thames, Westminster Abby, a few castles and then the short flight south."

We gazed at each other. "It seems wonderful, Kim. But what happens with my education? I'm sort of planning to eventually earn a Ph.D."

"Your education would continue. You see, my father still has another idea. He would like for you to study at the Sorbonne in Paris for a time. I would be enrolled in the best international school available. I will be 15 by then and should be able to take care of myself." She smiled.

"Is this what you want, Kim?"

"I think so. Don't you imagine it might be fun?"

"I think it might be wonderful. Do you think it could actually come to pass?"

"It will if my father has anything to say about it. He seems determined."

"I assume all four of us would be visiting the French capital for a few days. Following that, I imagine Lorna and your father would fly back to Denver, leaving the two of us in Paris in the springtime." I grinned. "Would you like my speech now, or later?"

"Oh, give it to me now, though I'm quite certain I know what you're going to say."

I smiled at her. "I am 19 now, Kim, and you are 14. Nobody knows what you'll be thinking in a year or two. But know this, Kim, while I always love being with you and am looking forward to our time together in Paris, just because we're in France in the springtime, doesn't mean you'll be having any sex, at least not with me."

She smiled. "Please remember what I told you when we were having our cheeseburgers and malts that last time. We go forward day by day. Didn't Lorna say something once, something about staying strong and moral? Maybe that's what we should strive for. Staying strong and moral."

I laughed. "Hearing you opt for staying strong and moral somehow causes me to shiver in my shoes. Actually though, Kim, what Lorna really said was: 'I hope to hell we never stay strong!' And this remains my problem to this very day. She usually hides her feelings quite well in a group, but when the two of us are alone all I get are icy stares."

"It really doesn't seem fair, though. Let's remember, she started it, and in my own bedroom!"

"True, but let's try and go a bit easy on her. Surely to God, she'll eventually get over me." I grinned. "And don't keep scaring her either."

"Actually I'm fascinated by Lorna. A part of me believes it's not you she longs for but me! Why else did she drag you into my bedroom? Didn't she say once, 'it has to be Kim's room'?"

"Yes I heard her say it!"

"Think it's possible she swings both ways?"

"Actually I don't think she knows what she wants."

Kim laughed. "Remember when Lorna kissed me that day in the hospital? As I recall the two of you were planning to stop for coffee on the way home."

"What kind of kiss did you give her that day, for God's sake?"

"A straight forward kiss, with just the tip of my tongue toward the end. Didn't get your coffee that day, did you?"

"I don't remember."

"The hell you don't!" Kim paused. "You're going to have a real battle with my 'play mother.' Maybe I should warn her and scare her to death. I don't like her bothering you."

"Oh, I don't know. Let's let the situation float along. I think I'll win the battle eventually."

Kim gazed at me. "I sure hope so," she said.

Three days later I had a serious discussion with Kim's father about the possible upcoming vacation plans for earlier the following year, and my study at the Sorbonne. He said he agreed with Kim's plans for the order of visiting the various countries, beginning with Italy, and added that he had already purchased good European maps for us to use on our travels.

He also insisted that my teaching sessions with Kim continue, though in all honesty most of what Kim was getting now were my notes from my present university classes. She appeared to take them seriously, though, and absorbed the information with the greatest of ease. Sometimes I think Kim is the one who should be studying at the Sorbonne.

My last question for Stan dealt with logistical factors. Do the two of us have the time? Who do you have to run your business for six or seven weeks? His answers were totally upbeat, and gave me the impression he was already beginning to concentrate on the trip itself.

Other aspects of our lives were continuing, of course, some of which had nothing to do with traveling in Europe. About six weeks after my parents returned from Hawaii they invited the Worthington family to their own home on a Sunday afternoon. It was another example of spotless behavior on the part of Kim. I'm beginning to think my young friend is growing up. Now if I can keep her from scaring Lorna to death all will be well.

It was Kim who spoke with me about visiting my university regarding our upcoming trip to Europe, suggesting she accompany me to our meeting in the registrar's office. I immediately saw why. She had in her hand three pages of detailed instructions from her father, outlining the steps needed to insure my enrollment in the University of Paris (the Sorbonne). Kim suggested I memorize Stan's pages before our meeting.

Later in the registrar's office we learned from the lady in

charge that I had complete flexibility as far as when I might return from Paris, or even if I would return. I did have the option of graduating from Denver later if I wished. It was at that early stage in the discussion that the lady across from us, whose name was Ms. Radcliff, glanced at Kim.

"And are you also planning to travel to Paris?"

"Yes, my father is placing me in an international school there. I've also planned our entire European tour. Paris will be our last stop. I will be 15 then, which means I can take care of myself."

"I'll bet you can," Ms. Radcliff said, more or less seriously.

"Of course, Michael will also be sort of looking after me. Although we don't know this for certain yet, it's possible by then I will be his legal ward."

The lady smiled. "I see. I suppose the French are quite up on such matters." It was quiet then in that office.

"Because of our schedule," I suggested, "I will not be attending our university here during the spring semester of next year. Our tour begins in late February."

Ms. Radcliff glanced at Kim pleasantly. "It appears you'll be reaching Paris in the springtime. How marvelous. I envy you."

"We might get robbed by Gypsies," Kim said, attempting to tone things down a little.

"Oh, maybe not. Let's hope for the best. But now, let's review a few matters. She turned her attention to me. "You, Mr. Sheppard, were the Valedictorian of your senior class, and have a full scholarship here in our university. As I said earlier, with your record, we will be highly flexible as far as your future plans are concerned. Also, I'm going to be speaking with both the president and the vice president. We will need letters of recommendation from both of them. If you wish, these letters could be sent to the Sorbonne in Paris in advance. We will also want to publicize your plans in various newspapers in Colorado. We will need photographs. You will also need copies of all your transcripts from this semester, as well as next fall. Should there be other members of our faculty who you believe should be writing letters of recommendation, you should alert our office. We'll take care of it."

Kim raised her hand. "I know your university covers students with their medical insurance. Could that coverage be extended to Michael for a year or two while he is at the Sorbonne in Paris?"

"An excellent question." Ms. Radcliff turned her attention to me. "Yes, Michael you would be covered for one additional year. Following that, you should probably arrange additional coverage with a private insurance company." It was suddenly quiet again in the office.

Radcliff had paused and was glancing at Kim again. "Excuse me, Ms. Worthington, but I've only just now recognized you. I've naturally read about you constantly in the Denver papers. While this is none of my business, I'm curious as to what finally happened to you. I was actually in the courtroom the day when your trial collapsed."

"It's all right. I don't mind answering your questions. You may remember that Michael refused to press charges. I was finally declared mentally incompetent and sentenced to nine months in the large mental facility on the South Platte River. After two months I was declared competent again and dismissed from the home. I argued with the committee of four about this because I felt I deserved a more-lengthy sentence. No one listened to me. I was told that this was a mental health facility and there was no room for any sane person hanging around taking up space. That's about the whole story." Kim and I were standing now and ready to leave. Ms. Radcliff, however, asked one additional question.

"Excuse me, but much of Denver is asking the same question. Why did you shoot Michael?"

Kim looked at her and smiled. "Frankly, he ticked me off that day. Thanks very much for your help Ms. Radcliff." We both waved goodbye.

Returning from the university I dropped Kim off on the east side of her home and was now parked in front of my own house, contemplating my own small universe, and drinking a couple of beers. Actually, eventually three beers.

At first I thought about Lorna and some of the problems she was facing. While I know her relationship with her husband appeared positive on the surface, her attitude toward me remained cool as snow in Siberia. As I told Kim earlier, in the presence of others she often faked her feelings of distaste, but when we were alone, she gave me nothing but the old evil eye.

I wondered if she ever considered what might have happened had we been caught. We would immediately have lost everything relating to the Worthington family. She would have been cut from any inheritance, and tossed out on her butt! I would have been sent packing as well. Kim would have stayed close to us, but only because she was still in love with me.

It seemed incredible to me that someone in their early twenties like Lorna could possibly have been willing to risk everything because of a roll in the hay, and had I been faced with the same situation again, I would have dug in my heals and turned her down, no matter how many times I broke her heart.

I should have realized that first evening that something was drastically wrong in that house. A woman who hadn't slept with her husband for more than two years, and who then dragged an 18-year-old college student into his girlfriend's bedroom in desperation; well, the more I thought about that evening, as well as the following morning, it became clear to me that Lorna had a strange fixation on Kim and, whether she admitted it or not, it fostered a dangerous situation for everyone concerned.

I don't know what is going on in that beautiful head of the girl from New Orleans, but I'm certain it can't be good. Anyway, I'm away from it now, though I'll admit, I still miss Lorna like crazy.

I've often wondered if there might be some danger to me personally, even though I'm no longer involved with Lorna. I suppose it depends on how deranged she becomes. The only weapon she might have is confessing everything to Kim's father in the middle of an out-of-control spasm of despair. That might be somewhat suicidal, however, because it might cause both Kim and Stan to turn against her. For this reason, I doubt she would risk such an attack on me.

Meanwhile, Lorna was trapped. Evidently she continued to fake it with her husband in bed, which can't be especially enjoyable, and she also had no real plan of escape. Without me as a partner, there doesn't seem to be any hope of running for it, whether to New Orleans, or some other place in the country. As I considered this, Lorna's position didn't seem much different than women in the 19th century who were trapped in the arms of their husbands, whether they liked it there or not. Good Lord, no wonder she had lured me into Kim's bedroom that evening. Anything except living with the status quo.

Kim had, in light-hearted fashion asked once, "she any good in bed?" I didn't answer her, of course, but had I given an honest reply, I would have said, "she was very sweet, and tried her best." That's exactly the way I remembered her. She certainly didn't need all my energy, but I still enjoyed being with her in a relaxed sort of way. Why she still seems taken with me is more than I can fathom. Frankly, I don't think I'm worth all the trouble.

Finally, after several more minutes sitting in my car, I opened my door, still carrying a last beer. But, instead of heading around to the right toward my front door, I turned left and walked into my yard on the east side.

I remembered the lawn party we had with Roberta and Paul Stipanovitch when Kim had raced down the hill on her scooter. I remembered further back, after my parents purchased this small house for me and I had been mowing this lawn for the first time. I remembered a young girl walking down that hill, wearing a Rockies cap sort of cockeyed, and carrying a baseball, which she threw at my head, missing me by less than a foot. She grabbed my small lawn mower then and started mowing the lawn herself, her father watching the scene from high on the hill. I took two or three more swigs of beer recalling this.

Walking up the hill later to her house, I did not meet either Stan Worthington or his wife that day, though Kim did show me a picture of Lorna, insisting it was her real mother and that this was what she would look like at age 17.

Kim often cursed and more often lied, and though I already knew she was in love with me that day, I had not a single card to play. She was 12 years old, though already running loose on the streets of Denver. Soon I would be hired to teach her English and history and control her in general, but that would turn out to be a very wild ride extending over several months.

That first day she showed me the Luger, insisting she purchased it from an old drunk near the mall, who had soon died lying next to a large garbage container. But there was a second weapon I had not seen that day. It was in a shoebox under her bed. It was a 22 semi-automatic, which no one knew a thing about except the old drunk, who really had sold her this weapon before he died. Her father was the one who purchased the little Luger.

Her parents, she said, were hippie types, often hopped up and out of control. She insisted her life was in such dire straits that I should soon attempt to adopt her, and that any judge would surely allow such a ruling. Of course, she insisted her parents didn't give a damn about her, and allowed her to run wild on the streets, her jeans filled with $50 bills. She said she seldom went to school, but did whatever she liked. She said she was like Huckleberry Finn, though a girl, of course. Once two policemen came to drag her back to school, but she had driven them both off with the Luger, which had real bullets that really stung. Lie, after lie, after lie.

On her 13th birthday I gave her a small kiss on the forehead, but she was not pleased, calling it a 'baby kiss.' I made a horrible mistake then kissing her full on the mouth and leading her to believe that if she played things right she might possibly get more of the same. She finally shot me!

Yes, shot me! Three times! Of course, she had her reasons. Lorna had seduced me by then, dragging me into Kim's own bedroom and taking advantage. As soon as Kim realized this, she yanked out the 22 and threatened the whole damned house! She almost shot Lorna, who I think actually deserved it, but she was lying there drugged up and so she didn't get the slug. I got three of the damned things!

Of course, Kim pleaded insanity and was placed in a mental institution for a while.

I took my last swig of beer and walked back to my house. After all of the violence we had experienced on Kim's part, and the sexual indiscretions on the part of Lorna and myself, we were now on the verge of flying off to Europe for a few weeks of self-cleansing. Lorna especially needed to free herself from me in terms of her sexual fantasies.

Before all this took place, however, due to the sudden death of Ben Zuckermann, the paperwork from his law office finally surfaced. I distinctly remembered our conversation that day in the hospital before Stan Worthington arrived, how Zuckermann had practically insisted I remain for the meeting about Kim's inheritance. It was the first time I heard about the $30,000,000 coming to Kim at age 20.

Before Stan's arrival I had asked Zuckermann about Lorna Worthington's mental condition, something he had brought up before. He stated that everything was still under consideration, including the mental stuff. This, of course, was typical lawyer's blather.

When Stan joined us, after we had our coffee and were seated at a large table in the cafeteria, his first words were, "Did you handle the situation with my wife?"

Zuckermann said he had reservations about the plan.

Stan insisted Lorna had her chance and that the lawyer should move forward. Stan then explained to me that they were discussing the situation with his wife.

I nodded, but made no comment. A little later, though I mentioned that Kim was quite fond of her stepmother.

"Exactly," the lawyer said, agreeing with me. "Let me warn you, Stan, nobody knows what will happen if you cut off Lorna's money. Hell, she might leave the state!"

"Perhaps, I just don't know. What do you think, Michael?"

"I'm not sure either. But if you really pass on, Stan, I know what the situation will be up on the hill. The two women will be stone cold broke!"

"How much money would they need for the seven years?"

"I'll have to think about it. Just remember, though, Kim has no money until age 20." I glanced at Zuckermann who was sitting there quietly shaking his head.

The conversation continued. After a while I didn't take it seriously. In short, I didn't believe Ben Zuckermann would ever bring me into a meaningful discussion regarding the family fortune.

But I was wrong! I had covered myself by calling Zuckermann about the $14,000,000 later but, after his death, everything came to light. The large sum was there in black and white. I was placed in charge of the whole damned place. Lorna was given no power whatsoever, and Kim was told to tow the line and listen to her boyfriend.

Back to the meeting itself, though, I soon gave up and excused myself to go upstairs and visit Kim. Unfortunately, I found her asleep, which led me back to the house on the hill and Lorna.

Of course, that entire meeting in the hospital cafeteria had been contingent on Stan's death. As of now, though, Stan seems quite healthy and ready to head out for Europe with the three of us. He's also had a complete change of heart about Lorna and joy is evident in every corner of the large home. Meanwhile, the weeks and months continued to slip away. Christmas and New Years had passed and it appeared our trip to Europe was actually going to come about.

Kim's plan of operation was still uppermost in our minds. In late winter we were in Italy, followed by Munich, Prague, Krakow and St. Petersburg. We had a bit of trouble in Italy, in Florence actually, when we were almost mugged getting back to our hotel. Kim's father drove the young man away by pulling the Luger out of his jacket pocket and aiming it at his head. The man had obviously thought it was a real gun. So far, so good.

Munich was marvelous, as was Prague. In Prague the buildings of the old Holy Roman Empire were being kept up in great fashion and we studied the history there in detail. I had never been to Krakow before and the architecture there enthralled me so much I thought I might one day change my major. Well, maybe not.

By the time we reached St. Petersburg it was obvious to me that Lorna was not going to alter her attitude toward me any time soon, giving me the same blank stares as she usually did. I tried being friendly, but she rejected my every move. Stan and Kim seemed deliriously happy and even Lorna faked it to a certain extent when we were visiting the various historical sites.

I had mentioned to Paul Stipanovitch earlier when he was living in Denver, that St. Petersburg was one of the most beautiful cities in the world, and asked why he'd left. He gave us the story of his girlfriend and their various problems, the same girl he had recently married. But St. Petersburg lived up to its billing and, even though we had a government official leading us around by our necks, I couldn't get enough of that eastern metropolis. We actually stayed eight days there and I believe we saw just about everything our official suggested.

And then there was London. Well, Americans are naturally fascinated by its architecture, history and the many castles available to visitors. We only stayed a week there, but I already knew I would one day return. During our entire trip I had done every bit of the driving, but now I had a real challenge on my hands. I was forced to drive on the wrong side of the road! It took me an entire day to get used to it.

Paris was as beautiful as I remembered it. It was now spring-time there and, although we stayed an entire week, I know Stan and Lorna didn't see half of what they should have. There was one break-through with Lorna, though. We were walking near the Eifel Tower one afternoon when she gave me a real smile. I smiled back, hoping this might be the beginning of a thaw. But one thing would not change. No matter how many times she walked down that hill to my house, all she would ever get from me was a can of cold pop!

The paperwork for Kim and myself had long since been turned into the two educational institutions—the Sorbonne for me, and the best international school in Paris for Kim. We've already had our vacation in Europe and so Monday morning we will both be back in school. The two of us have our own apartments there in the middle of Paris, paid for by Stan Worthington, plus a bank account for the two of us to draw on.

Friday afternoon the four of us took a taxi to Charles De Gaulle International Airport and we said goodbye to Stan and Lorna and watched as their plane eventually took off, heading home to America. Kim and I looked seriously at each other for a few seconds, realizing we had been left alone in Europe. We soon gave each other a bright smile, though and took another taxi back to the middle of the city.

We were on the Champs Elysees a few hundred yards down from the Arc de Triomphe when I glanced at Kim suddenly, somewhat in astonishment. She is 15 years old now and, no matter what happens in her life in the future, she will never be more beautiful than she is today.

She looked up at me then and saw I was grinning. "I have a question," she said. "Do you think the French would mind if we walked together hand-in-hand here in Paris?"

"No, Kim," I said. "I really don't think the French would mind at all." I took her hand and we walked on together.

**About the Author:**

Dr. James Paulding has taught more than 30 years at the university level in Illinois and Missouri, as well as directing a band for the United States Seventh Army in Europe. *The Kissing Law* is his 9th published book. He and his wife, Helga, have also created three documentary films, the last being *Brothers in the Storm*. They alternate between living in the Denver area and central Europe, including Germany, Austria and the Czech Republic.